Kazuo Ishiguro was born in Nagasaki, Japan, in 1954 and came to Britain at the age of five. He is the author of five novels: *A Pale View of Hills* (1982, Winifred Holtby Prize), *An Artist of the Floating World* (1986, Whitbread Book of the Year Award, Premio Scanno, shortlisted for the Booker Prize), *The Remains of the Day* (1989, winner of the Booker Prize) and *The Unconsoled* (1995, winner of the Cheltenham Prize) and *When We Were Orphans* (shortlisted for both the Booker Prize and Whitbread Prize 2000).

Kazuo Ishiguro's work has been translated into twenty-eight languages. *The Remains of the Day* became an international bestseller, with over a million copies sold in the English language alone, and was adapted into an award-winning film starring Anthony Hopkins and Emma Thompson.

In 1995 Ishiguro received an OBE for Services to Literature, and in 1998 the French decoration of Chevalier de l'Ordre des Arts et Lettres. He lives in London with his wife and daughter.

by the same author

A PALE VIEW OF HILLS
THE REMAINS OF THE DAY
THE UNCONSOLED
WHEN WE WERE ORPHANS

KAZUO ISHIGURO

An Artist of
the Floating World

faber and faber

First published in 1986
by Faber and Faber Limited
3 Queen Square London WC1N 3AU
First published in paperback in 1987
This edition first published in 2001

Photoset by Parker Typesetting Service, Leicester
Printed in England by
Mackays of Chatham plc, Chatham, Kent

The right of Kazuo Ishiguro to be identified as the author of
this work has been asserted in accordance with Section 77
of the Copyright, Designs and Patents Act 1988

A CIP record for this book
is available from the British Library

ISBN 0-571-20913-0

2 4 6 8 10 9 7 5 3 1

OCTOBER, 1948

If on a sunny day you climb the steep path leading up from the little wooden bridge still referred to around here as 'the Bridge of Hesitation', you will not have to walk far before the roof of my house becomes visible between the tops of two gingko trees. Even if it did not occupy such a commanding position on the hill, the house would still stand out from all others nearby, so that as you come up the path, you may find yourself wondering what sort of wealthy man owns it.

But then I am not, nor have I ever been, a wealthy man. The imposing air of the house will be accounted for, perhaps, if I inform you that it was built by my predecessor, and that he was none other than Akira Sugimura. Of course, you may be new to this city, in which case the name of Akira Sugimura may not be familiar to you. But mention it to anyone who lived here before the war and you will learn that for thirty years or so, Sugimura was unquestionably amongst the city's most respected and influential men.

If I tell you this, and when arriving at the top of the hill you stand and look at the fine cedar gateway, the large area bound by the garden wall, the roof with its elegant tiles and its stylishly carved ridgepole pointing out over the view, you may well wonder how I came to acquire such a property, being as I claim a man of only moderate means. The truth is, I bought the house for a nominal sum – a figure probably not even half the property's true value at that time. This was made possible owing to a most curious – some may say foolish – procedure instigated by the Sugimura family during the sale.

It is now already a thing of some fifteen years ago. In those days, when my circumstances seemed to improve with each month, my wife had begun to press me to find a new house. With her usual foresight, she had argued the importance of our having a house in keeping with our status – not out of vanity, but for the sake of our children's marriage prospects. I saw the sense in this, but since Setsuko, our eldest, was still only fourteen or fifteen, I did not go about the matter with any urgency. Nevertheless, for a year or so, whenever I heard of a suitable house for sale, I would remember to make enquiries. It was one of my pupils who first brought it to my attention that Akira Sugimura's house, a year after his death, was to be sold off. That I should buy such a house seemed absurd, and I put the suggestion down to the exaggerated respect my pupils always had for me. But I made enquiries all the same, and gained an unexpected response.

I received a visit one afternoon from two haughty, grey-haired ladies, who turned out to be the daughters of Akira Sugimura. When I expressed my surprise at receiving such personal attention from a family of such distinction, the elder of the sisters told me coldly that they had not come simply out of courtesy. Over the previous months, a fair number of enquiries had been received for their late father's house, but the family had in the end decided to refuse all but four of the applications. These four applicants had been selected carefully by family members on grounds purely of good character and achievement.

'It is of the first importance to us', she went on, 'that the house our father built should pass to one he would have approved of and deemed worthy of it. Of course, circumstances oblige us to consider the financial aspect, but this is strictly secondary. We have therefore set a price.'

At this point, the younger sister, who had barely spoken, presented me with an envelope, and they watched me sternly as I opened it. Inside was a single sheet of paper, blank but for a figure written elegantly with an ink brush. I was about to express my astonishment at the low price, but then saw from the faces before me that further discussion of finances would be considered distasteful. The elder sister said simply: 'It will not be in the interests of any of you to try to outbid one another. We are not interested in receiving anything beyond the quoted price. What we mean to do from here on is to conduct an auction of prestige.'

They had come in person, she explained, to ask formally on behalf of the Sugimura family that I submit myself – along, of course, with the other three applicants – to a closer investigation of my background and credentials. A suitable buyer could thus be chosen.

It was an eccentric procedure, but I saw nothing objectionable about it; it was, after all, much the same as being involved in a marriage negotiation. Indeed, I felt somewhat flattered to be considered by this old and hidebound family as a worthy candidate. When I gave my consent to the investigation, and expressed my gratitude to them, the younger sister addressed me for the first time, saying: 'Our father was a cultured man, Mr Ono. He had much respect for artists. Indeed, he knew of your work.'

In the days which followed, I made enquiries of my own, and discovered the truth of the younger sister's words; Akira Sugimura had indeed been something of an art enthusiast who on numerous occasions had supported exhibitions with his money. I also came across certain interesting rumours: a significant section of the Sugimura family, it seemed, had been against selling the house at all, and there had been some bitter arguments. In the end, financial pressures meant a sale was inevitable, and the odd procedures around the transaction represented the compromise reached with those who had not wished the house to pass out of the family. That there was something high-handed about these arrangements there was no denying; but for my part, I was prepared to sympathize with the sentiments of a family with such a distinguished history. My wife, however, did not take kindly to the idea of an investigation.

'Who do they think they are?' she protested. 'We should

tell them we want nothing further to do with them.'

'But where's the harm?' I pointed out. 'We have nothing we wouldn't want them to discover. True, I don't have a wealthy background, but no doubt the Sugimuras know that already, and they still think us worthy candidates. Let them investigate, they can only find things that will be to our advantage.' And I made a point of adding: 'In any case, they're doing no more than they would if we were negotiating a marriage with them. We'll have to get used to this sort of thing.'

Besides, there was surely much to admire in the idea of 'an auction of prestige', as the elder daughter called it. One wonders why things are not settled more often by such means. How so much more honourable is such a contest, in which one's moral conduct and achievement are brought as witnesses rather than the size of one's purse. I can still recall the deep satisfaction I felt when I learnt the Sugimuras – after the most thorough investigation – had deemed me the most worthy of the house they so prized. And certainly, the house is one worth having suffered a few inconveniences for; despite its impressive and imposing exterior, it is inside a place of soft, natural woods selected for the beauty of their grains, and all of us who lived in it came to find it most conducive to relaxation and calm.

For all that, the Sugimuras' high-handedness was apparent everywhere during the transactions, some family members making no attempts to hide their hostility towards us, and a less understanding buyer might well have taken offence and abandoned the whole matter. Even in later years I would sometimes encounter by chance some member of the family who, instead of exchanging the usual kind of polite talk, would stand there in the street interrogating me as to the state of the house and any alterations I had made.

These days, I hardly ever hear of the Sugimuras. I did, though, receive a visit shortly after the surrender from the younger of the two sisters who had approached me at the time of the sale. The war years had turned her into a thin, ailing old woman. In the way characteristic of the family, she made scant effort to hide the fact that her concern lay with how the house – rather than its inhabitants – had fared during the war; she gave only the briefest of commiserations on hearing about my wife and about Kenji, before embarking on questions concerning the bomb damage. This made me bitter towards her at first; but then I began to notice how her eyes would roam involuntarily around the room, and how she would occasionally pause abruptly in the midst of one of her measured and formal sentences, and I realized she was experiencing waves of emotion at finding herself back in this house once more. Then, when I surmised that most of her family members from the time of the sale were now dead, I began to feel pity for her and offered to show her around.

The house had received its share of the war damage. Akira Sugimura had built an eastern wing to the house, comprising three large rooms, connected to the main body of the house by a long corridor running down one side of the garden. This corridor was so extravagant in its length that some people have suggested Sugimura built it – together with the east wing – for his parents, whom he wished to keep at a distance. The corridor was, in any case, one of the most appealing features of the house; in the afternoon, its entire length would be crossed by the lights and shades of the foliage outside, so that one felt one was walking through a garden tunnel. The bulk of the bomb damage had been to this section of the house, and as we surveyed it from the garden I could see Miss Sugimura was close to tears. By this point, I had lost all my earlier sense of irritation with the old woman and I reassured her as best I could that the damage would be repaired at the first opportunity, and the house would be once more as her father had built it.

I had no idea when I promised her this that supplies would remain so scarce. For a long time after the surrender one could wait weeks just for a particular piece of wood or a supply of nails. What work I could do under such circumstances had to be done to the main body of the house – which had by no means entirely escaped damage – and progress on the garden corridor and the east wing has been slow. I have done what I can to prevent any serious deterioration, but we are still far from being able to open that part of the house again. Besides, now with only Noriko and myself left here, there seems less urgency to be extending our living space.

Today, if I took you to the back of the house, and moved aside the heavy screen to let you gaze down the remains of Sugimura's garden corridor, you may still gain an impression of how picturesque it once was. But no doubt you will notice too the cobwebs and mould that I have not been able to keep out; and the large gaps in the ceiling, shielded from the sky only by sheets of tarpaulin. Sometimes, in the early morning, I have moved back that screen to find the sunlight pouring through the tarpaulin in tinted shafts, revealing clouds of dust hanging in the air as though the ceiling had only that moment crashed down.

Aside from the corridor and the east wing, the most serious damage was to the veranda. Members of my family, and particularly my two daughters, had always been fond of passing the time sitting there, chatting and viewing the garden; and so, when Setsuko – my married daughter – first came to visit us after the surrender, I was not surprised to see how saddened she was by its condition. I had by then repaired the worst of the damage, but at one end it was still billowed and cracked where the impact of the blast had pushed up the boards from underneath. The veranda roof, too, had suffered, and on rainy days we were still having to line the floorboards with receptacles to catch the water that came dripping through.

Over this past year, however, I was able to make a certain amount of progress, and by the time Setsuko came down to visit us again last month, the veranda was more or less entirely restored. Noriko had taken time off work for her sister's visit, and so, with the good weather continuing, my two daughters spent a lot of their time out there as of old. I often joined them, and at times it was almost as it had been years ago, when on a sunny day the family would sit there together exchanging relaxed, often vacuous talk. At one point last month – it must have been the first morning after Setsuko's arrival – we were sitting there on the veranda after breakfast, when Noriko said:

'I'm relieved you've come at last, Setsuko. You'll take Father off my hands a little.'

'Noriko, really . . .' Her elder sister shifted uncomfortably on her cushion.

'Father takes a lot of looking after now he's retired,' Noriko went on, with a mischievous grin. 'You've got to keep him occupied or he starts to mope.'

'Really . . .' Setsuko smiled nervously, then turned to the garden with a sigh. 'The maple tree seems to have recovered completely. It's looking splendid.'

'Setsuko probably has no idea of what you're like these days, Father. She only remembers you from when you were a tyrant and ordered us all around. You're much more gentle these days, isn't that so?'

I gave a laugh to show Setsuko this was all in good humour, but my elder daughter continued to look uncomfortable. Noriko turned back to her sister and added: 'But he does take a lot more looking after, moping around the house all day.'

'She's talking nonsense as usual,' I put in. 'If I spend the whole day moping, how did all these repairs get done?'

'Indeed,' Setsuko said, turning to me and smiling. 'The house is looking marvellous now. Father must have worked very hard.'

'He had men in to help with all the difficult parts,' Noriko said. 'You don't seem to believe me, Setsuko. Father's very different now. There's no need to be afraid of him any more. He's much more gentle and domesticated.'

'Noriko, really . . .'

'He even cooks meals from time to time. You wouldn't have

13

believed it, would you? But Father's becoming a much better cook these days.'

'Noriko, I think we've discussed this enough,' Setsuko said, quietly.

'Isn't that so, Father? You're making a lot of progress.'

I gave another smile and shook my head wearily. It was at that point, as I remember, that Noriko turned towards the garden, and closing her eyes to the sunshine, said:

'Well, he can't rely on me to come back and cook when I'm married. I'll have enough to do without Father to look after as well.'

As Noriko said this, her elder sister – whose gaze until then had been demurely turned away – gave me a swift, enquiring look. Her eyes left me again immediately, for she was obliged to return Noriko's smile. But a new, more profound uneasiness had entered Setsuko's manner and she seemed grateful when her little boy, speeding past us down the veranda, gave her an opportunity to change the subject.

'Ichiro, please settle!' she called after him.

No doubt, after the modern apartment of his parents, Ichiro was fascinated by the large amount of space in our house. In any case, he seemed not to share our fondness for sitting on the veranda, preferring instead to run at great speed up and down its length, sometimes sliding along the polished boards. More than once, he had come close to upsetting our tea tray, but his mother's requests that he sit down had so far been to little avail. This time too, when Setsuko called to him to take a cushion with us, he remained sulking at the end of the veranda.

'Come on, Ichiro,' I called out, 'I'm tired of talking to women all the time. You come and sit beside me and we'll talk about men's things.'

This brought him straight away. He placed his cushion next to me, then seated himself in a most noble posture, hands on hips, his shoulders flung well back.

'Oji,' he said to me sternly, 'I have a question.'

14

'Yes, Ichiro, what is it?'

'I want to know about the monster.'

'The monster?'

'Is it prehistoric?'

'Prehistoric? You know words like that already? You must be a clever boy.'

At this point, Ichiro's dignity seemed to give way. Abandoning his pose, he rolled on to his back and began waving his feet in the air.

'Ichiro!' Setsuko called in an urgent whisper. 'Such bad manners in front of your grandfather. Sit up!'

Ichiro's only response was to allow his feet to slump lifelessly on to the floorboards. He then folded his arms over his chest and closed his eyes.

'Oji,' he said, in a sleepy voice, 'is the monster prehistoric?'

'Which monster is this, Ichiro?'

'Please excuse him,' Setsuko said, with a nervous smile. 'There was a film poster outside the railway station when we arrived yesterday. He inconvenienced the taxi driver with numerous questions. It's so unfortunate I didn't see the poster myself.'

'Oji! Is the monster prehistoric or isn't it? I want an answer!'

'Ichiro!' His mother gave him a horrified look.

'I'm not sure, Ichiro. I should think we have to see the film to find out.'

'When do we see the film then?'

'Hmm. You'd best discuss it with your mother. You never know, it may be too frightening for young children.'

I had not meant this remark to be provocative, but its effect on my grandson was startling. He rolled back into a sitting position and glared at me, shouting: 'How dare you! What are you saying!'

'Ichiro!' Setsuko exclaimed in dismay. But Ichiro continued to regard me with the most fearsome look, and his mother

15

was obliged to leave her cushion to come over to us. 'Ichiro!' she whispered to him, shaking his arm. 'Don't stare at your grandfather like that.'

Ichiro responded by falling on to his back again and waving his feet in the air. His mother gave me another nervous smile.

'So bad-mannered,' she said. Then seemingly at a loss for further words, she smiled again.

'Ichiro-san,' Noriko said, getting to her feet, 'why don't you come and help me put away the breakfast things?'

'Women's work,' Ichiro said, his feet still waving.

'So Ichiro won't help me? Now that's a problem. The table's so heavy I'm not strong enough to put that away on my own. I wonder who could help then?'

This brought Ichiro abruptly to his feet, and he went striding indoors without glancing back at us. Noriko laughed and followed him in.

Setsuko glanced after them, then lifting the teapot, began refilling my cup. 'I had no idea things had come so far,' she said, her voice lowered. 'I mean as regards Noriko's marriage negotiations.'

'Things haven't come far at all,' I said, shaking my head. 'In fact, nothing's settled at all. We're still at an early stage.'

'Forgive me, but from what Noriko said just a moment ago, I naturally supposed things were more or less . . .' She trailed off, then said again: 'Forgive me.' But she said it in such a way that a question was left hanging in the air.

'I'm afraid this isn't the first time Noriko's spoken like that,' I said. 'In fact, she's been behaving oddly ever since these present negotiations began. Last week, we had a visit from Mr Mori – you remember him?'

'Of course. He's well?'

'Well enough. He was just passing and called to pay his respects. The point is, Noriko began to talk about the marriage negotiations in front of him. She took much the same attitude as just now, that everything was settled. It was most embarrassing. Mr Mori even congratulated me as he was leaving, and asked me the groom's occupation.'

'Indeed,' Setsuko said, thoughtfully. 'It must have been embarrassing.'

'But it was hardly Mr Mori's fault. You heard her yourself just now. What was a stranger supposed to think?'

My daughter did not reply, and we sat there in silence for a few moments. Once, when I glanced over at her, Setsuko was gazing out at the garden, holding her teacup in both hands as though she had forgotten it was there. It was one of several occasions during her visit last month when – perhaps because of the way the light caught her, or some such thing – I found myself contemplating her appearance. For there can be no doubt, Setsuko is becoming better looking as she gets older. In her youth, her mother and I had worried that she was too plain to make a good marriage. Even as a child, Setsuko had rather masculine features, which seemed only to grow more pronounced with adolescence; so much so that whenever my daughters quarrelled, Noriko was always able to get the better of her elder sister by calling her 'Boy! Boy!' Who knows what effect such things have on personalities? It is no coincidence, surely, that Noriko should have grown up so headstrong, and Setsuko so shy and retiring. But now, it seems, as she approaches her thirties, Setsuko's looks are taking on a new and not inconsiderable dignity. I can recall her mother predicting this – 'Our Setsuko will flower in the summer,' she had often said. I had thought this merely my wife's way of consoling herself, but then several times last month, I was struck by how correct she in fact had been.

Setsuko came out of her reverie, and cast another glance inside the house. Then she said: 'I would suppose what happened last year greatly upset Noriko. Much more perhaps than we supposed.'

I gave a sigh and nodded. 'It's possible I didn't pay enough attention to her at the time.'

'I'm sure Father did all he could. But of course, such things are a terrible blow to a woman.'

'I have to admit, I thought she was play-acting a little, the way your sister does sometimes. She'd been insisting it was a "love match", so when it fell through, she'd be obliged to behave accordingly. But perhaps it wasn't all play-acting.'

'We laughed at the time,' Setsuko said, 'but perhaps it really was a love match.'

We fell silent again. From inside the house, we could hear Ichiro's voice shouting something repeatedly.

'Forgive me,' Setsuko said, in a new voice. 'But did we ever hear any further as to why the proposal fell through last year? It was so unexpected.'

'I have no idea. It hardly matters now, does it?'

'Of course not, forgive me.' Setsuko seemed to consider something for a moment, then she spoke again: 'It's just that Suichi persists in asking me from time to time about last year, about why the Miyakes should have pulled out like that.' She gave a little laugh, almost to herself. 'He seems convinced I know some secret and that we're all keeping it from him. I have to continually reassure him that I have no idea myself.'

'I assure you,' I said a little coldly, 'it remains equally a mystery to me. If I knew, I wouldn't keep it from you and Suichi.'

'Of course. Please excuse me, I didn't mean to imply . . .' Again, she trailed off awkwardly.

I may have appeared a little short with my daughter that morning, but then that was not the first time Setsuko had questioned me in such a way concerning last year and the Miyakes' withdrawal. Why she should believe I am keeping something from her, I do not know. If the Miyakes had some special reason for withdrawing like that, it would stand to reason they would not confide in me about it.

My own guess is that there was nothing so remarkable about the matter. True, their withdrawal at the last moment was most unexpected, but why should one suppose from this that there was anything peculiar in it? My feeling is that it was simply a matter of family status. The Miyakes, from what I saw of them, were just the proud, honest sort who would feel uncomfortable at the thought of their son marrying above his station. Indeed, a few years ago, they would probably have withdrawn more promptly, but what with the couple claiming it was a 'love match', and with all the talk these days of the new ways, the Miyakes are the kind of people who would become confused as to their correct course. No doubt the explanation is no more complicated than that.

It is possible, too, that they were confused by my apparent approval of the match. For I was very lax in considering the matter of status, it simply not being my instinct to concern myself with such things. Indeed, I have never at any point in my life been very aware of my own social standing, and even now, I am often surprised afresh when some event, or something someone may say, reminds me of the rather high esteem in which I am held. Just the other evening, for instance, I was down in our old pleasure district, drinking at Mrs Kawakami's place, where – as happens increasingly these days – Shintaro and I had found ourselves the only customers. We were as usual sitting up at the bar on our high-stools, exchanging remarks with Mrs Kawakami, and as the hours had gone by, and no one else had come in, our exchanges had grown more intimate. At one point, Mrs Kawakami was talking about some relative of hers, complaining that the young man had been unable to find a job worthy of his abilities, when Shintaro suddenly exclaimed:

'You must send him to Sensei here, Obasan! A good word from Sensei in the right place, your relative will soon find a good post.'

'What are you saying, Shintaro?' I protested. 'I'm retired now. I have no connections these days.'

'A recommendation from a man of Sensei's standing will command respect from anyone,' Shintaro had persisted. 'Send the young man to Sensei, Obasan.'

I was at first a little taken aback by the conviction of Shintaro's assertions. But then I realized he was remembering yet again that small deed I had performed for his younger brother all those years ago.

It must have been in 1935 or 1936, a very routine matter as I recall – a letter of recommendation to an acquaintance in the State Department, some such thing. I would have given the matter little further thought, but then one afternoon while I was relaxing at home, my wife announced there were visitors for me at the entryway.

'Please show them in,' I had said.

'But they insist they won't bother you by coming in.'

I went out to the entryway, and standing there were Shintaro and his younger brother – then no more than a youth. As soon as they saw me, they began bowing and giggling.

'Please step up,' I said, but they continued simply to bow and giggle. 'Shintaro, please. Step up to the tatami.'

'No, Sensei,' Shintaro said, all the time smiling and bowing. 'It is the height of impertinence for us to come to your house like this. The height of impertinence. But we could not remain at home any longer without thanking you.'

'Come on inside. I believe Setsuko was just making some tea.'

'No, Sensei, it is the height of impertinence. Really.' Then turning to his brother, Shintaro whispered quickly: 'Yoshio! Yoshio!'

For the first time, the young man stopped bowing and looked up at me nervously. Then he said: 'I will be grateful to you for the remainder of my life. I will exert every particle of my being to be worthy of your recommendation. I assure you, I will not let you down. I will work hard, and strive to satisfy my superiors. And however much I may be promoted in the future, I will never forget the man who enabled me to start on my career.'

'Really, it was nothing. It's no more than you deserve.'

This brought frantic protests from both of them, then Shintaro said to his brother: 'Yoshio, we have imposed enough on Sensei as it is. But before we leave, take a good look again at

20

the man who has helped you. We are greatly privileged to have a benefactor of such influence and generosity.'

'Indeed,' the youth muttered, and gazed up at me.

'Please, Shintaro, this is embarrassing. Please come in and we'll celebrate with some sake.'

'No, Sensei, we must leave you now. It was the greatest impertinence to come here like this and disturb your afternoon. But we could not delay thanking you for one moment longer.'

This visit – I must admit it – left me with a certain feeling of achievement. It was one of those moments, in the midst of a busy career allowing little chance for stopping and taking stock, which illuminate suddenly just how far one has come. For true enough, I had almost unthinkingly started a young man on a good career. A few years earlier, such a thing would have been inconceivable and yet I had brought myself to such a position almost without realizing it.

'Many things have changed since the old days, Shintaro,' I pointed out the other night down at Mrs Kawakami's. 'I'm retired now, I don't have so many connections.'

But then for all I know, Shintaro may not be so wrong in his assumptions. It may be that if I chose to put it to the test, I would again be surprised by the extent of my influence. As I say, I have never had a keen awareness of my own standing.

In any case, even if Shintaro may at times display naïveté about certain things, this is nothing to be disparaged, it being no easy thing now to come across someone so untainted by the cynicism and bitterness of our day. There is something reassuring about going into Mrs Kawakami's and finding Shintaro sitting up there at the bar, just as one may have found him on any evening for the past seventeen or so years, absent-mindedly turning his cap round and round on the counter in that old way of his. It really is as though nothing has changed for Shintaro. He will greet me very politely, as though he were still my pupil, and throughout the evening, however drunk he may get, he will continue to address me as

'Sensei' and maintain his most respectful manner towards me. Sometimes he will even ask me questions relating to technique or style with all the eagerness of a young apprentice – though the truth is, of course, Shintaro has long ceased to be concerned with any real art. For some years now, he has devoted his time to his book illustrations, and his present speciality, I gather, is fire engines. He will work day after day up in that attic room of his, sketching out fire engine after fire engine. But I suppose in the evenings, after a few drinks, Shintaro likes to believe he is still the idealistic young artist I first took under my supervision.

This childlike aspect of Shintaro has frequently been a source of entertainment for Mrs Kawakami, who has a some-what wicked side to her. One night recently, for instance, during a rainstorm, Shintaro had come running into the little bar and begun squeezing his cap out over the doormat.

'Really, Shintaro-san!' Mrs Kawakami had shouted at him. 'What terrible manners!'

At this, Shintaro had looked up in great distress, as though indeed he had committed an outrageous offence. He had then begun to apologize profusely, thus leading Mrs Kawakami on further.

'I've never seen such manners, Shintaro-san. You seem to have no respect for me at all.'

'Now stop this, Obasan,' I had appealed to her after a while. 'That's enough, tell him you're just joking.'

'Joking? I'm hardly joking. The height of bad manners.'

And so it had gone on, until Shintaro had become quite pitiful to watch. But then again, on other occasions, Shintaro will be convinced he is being teased when in fact he is being spoken to quite earnestly. There was the time he had put Mrs Kawakami in difficulties by declaring cheerfully of a general who had just been executed as a war criminal: 'I've always admired that man since I was a boy. I wonder what he's up to now. Retired, no doubt.'

Some new customers had been present that night and had

looked at him disapprovingly. When Mrs Kawakami, concerned for her trade, had gone to him and told him quietly of the general's fate, Shintaro had burst out laughing.

'Really, Obasan,' he had said loudly. 'Some of your jokes are quite extreme.'

Shintaro's ignorance of such matters is often remarkable, but as I say, it is not something to disparage. One should be thankful there are still those uncontaminated by the current cynicism. In fact, it is probably this very quality of Shintaro's – this sense that he has remained somehow unscathed by things – which has led me to enjoy his company more and more over these recent years.

As for Mrs Kawakami, although she will do her best not to allow the current mood to affect her, there is no denying she has been greatly aged by the war years. Before the war, she may still have passed for a 'young woman', but since then something inside her seems to have broken and sagged. And when one remembers those she has lost in the war, it is hardly any wonder. Business too has become increasingly difficult for her; certainly, it must be hard for her to believe this is the same district where she first opened her little place those sixteen or seventeen years ago. For nothing really remains of our old pleasure district now; almost all her old competitors have closed up and left, and Mrs Kawakami must more than once have considered doing likewise.

But when her place first appeared, it was squeezed in amidst so many other bars and eating houses, I remember some people doubting if it could survive long. Indeed, you could hardly walk down those little streets without brushing against the numerous cloth banners pressing at you from all sides, leaning out at you from their shop fronts, each declaring the attractions of their establishment in boisterous lettering. But in those days, there was enough custom in the district to keep any number of such establishments thriving. On the warmer evenings particularly, the area would fill with people strolling unhurriedly from bar to bar, or just standing talking in the middle of the street. Cars had long ceased to venture through, and even a bicycle could only be pushed with difficulty past those throngs of uncaring pedestrians.

I say 'our pleasure district', but I suppose it was really nothing more than somewhere to drink, eat and talk. You would have had to go into the city centre for the real pleasure quarters – for the geisha houses and theatres. For myself though, our own district was always preferable. It drew a lively but respectable crowd, many of them people like us – artists and writers lured by the promise of noisy conversations continuing into the night. The establishment my own group frequented was called 'Migi-Hidari', and stood at a point where three side streets intersected to form a paved precinct. The Migi-Hidari, unlike any of its neighbours, was a large sprawling place with an upper floor and plenty of hostesses both in Western and traditional dress. I had played my own small part in the Migi-Hidari's coming to so dwarf its competitors, and in recognition of this, our group had been provided with a table in one corner for our sole use. Those who drank with me there were, in effect, the élite of my school: Kuroda, Murasaki, Tanaka – brilliant young men, already with growing reputations. They all of them relished conversation, and I remember many passionate arguments taking place around that table.

Shintaro, I should say, was never one of that select group. I would not myself have objected to his joining us, but there existed a strong sense of hierarchy amongst my pupils, and Shintaro was certainly not regarded as of the first rank. In fact, I can recall one night, shortly after Shintaro and his brother had paid that visit to my house, my discussing that episode around our table. I remember the likes of Kuroda laughing at how grateful the brothers had been over 'a mere white-collar appointment'; but then they all listened solemnly as I recounted my view on how influence and status can creep up on someone who works busily, not pursuing these ends in themselves, but for the satisfaction of performing his tasks to the best of his ability. At this point, one of them – no doubt it was Kuroda – leaned forward and said:

'I have suspected for some time that Sensei was unaware of the high regard in which he is held by people in this city. Indeed, as the instance he has just related amply illustrates, his reputation has now spread beyond the world of art, to all walks of life. But how typical of Sensei's modest nature that he is unaware of this. How typical that he himself should be the most surprised by the esteem accorded to him. But to all of us here it comes as no surprise. In fact, it may be said that respected enormously as he is by the public at large, it is we here at this table who alone know the extent to which that respect still falls short. But I personally have no doubt. His reputation will become all the greater, and in years to come, our proudest honour will be to tell others that we were once the pupils of Masuji Ono.'

Now there was nothing remarkable in all this; it had become something of a habit that at some point in the evening, when we had all drunk a little, my protégés would take to making speeches of a loyal nature to me. And Kuroda in particular, being looked on as a sort of spokesman for them, gave a fair proportion of these. Of course, I usually ignored them, but on this particular occasion, as when Shintaro and his brother had stood bowing and giggling in my entryway, I experienced a warm glow of satisfaction.

But then it would not be accurate to suggest I only socialized with the best of my pupils. Indeed, the first time I ever stepped into Mrs Kawakami's, I believe I did so because I wished to spend the evening talking something over with Shintaro. Today, when I try to recall that evening, I find my memory of it merging with the sounds and images from all those other evenings; the lanterns hung above doorways, the laughter of people congregated outside the Migi-Hidari, the smell of deep-fried food, a bar hostess persuading someone to return to his wife – and echoing from every direction, the clicking of numerous wooden sandals on the concrete. I remember it being a warm summer's night, and not finding Shintaro in his usual haunts, I wandered around those tiny bars for some time. For all the competition there must have existed between those establishments, a neighbourly spirit reigned, and it was quite natural that on asking after Shintaro at one such bar that night, I should be advised by the hostess, without a trace of resentment, to try for him at the 'new place'.

No doubt, Mrs Kawakami could point out numerous changes – her little 'improvements' – that she has made over the years. But my impression is that her little place looked much the same that first night as it does today. On entering, one tends to be struck by the contrast between the bar counter, lit up by warm, low-hung lights, and the rest of the room, which is in shadow. Most of her customers prefer to sit up at the bar within that pool of light, and this gives a cosy, intimate feel to the place. I remember looking around me with approval that first night, and today, for all the changes which have transformed the world around it, Mrs Kawakami's remains as pleasing as ever.

But little else has remained unchanged. Coming out of Mrs Kawakami's now, you could stand at her doorway and believe you have just been drinking at some outpost of civilization. All around, there is nothing but a desert of demolished rubble. Only the backs of several buildings far in the distance will remind you that you are not so far from the city centre. 'War damage,' Mrs Kawakami calls it. But I remember walking around the district shortly after the surrender and many of those buildings were still standing. The Migi-Hidari was still there, the windows all blown out, part of the roof fallen in. And I remember wondering to myself as I walked past those shattered buildings, if they would ever again come back to life. Then I came by one morning and the bulldozers had pulled down everything.

So now that side of the street is nothing but rubble. No doubt the authorities have their plans, but it has been that way for three years. The rain collects in small puddles and grows stagnant amidst the broken brick. As a consequence, Mrs Kawakami has been obliged to put up mosquito wiring on her windows – not an effect she thinks will attract customers.

The buildings on Mrs Kawakami's own side of the street have remained standing, but many are unoccupied; the properties on either side of her, for instance, have been vacant for some time, a situation which makes her uncomfortable. If she became suddenly rich, she often tells us, she would buy up those properties and expand. In the meantime, she waits for someone to move into them; she would not mind if they became bars just like hers, anything provided she no longer had to live in the midst of a graveyard.

If you were to come out of Mrs Kawakami's as the darkness was setting in, you might feel compelled to pause a moment and gaze at that wasted expanse before you. You might still be able to make out through the gloom those heaps of broken brick and timber, and perhaps here and there, pieces of piping protruding from the ground like weeds. Then as you walked on past more heaps of rubble, numerous small puddles would gleam a moment as they caught in the lamplight.

And if on reaching the foot of the hill which climbs up to my house, you pause at the Bridge of Hesitation and look back towards the remains of our old pleasure district, if the sun has not yet set completely, you may see the line of old telegraph poles – still without wires to connect them – disappearing into the gloom down the route you have just come, And you may be able to make out the dark clusters of birds perched uncomfortably on the tops of the poles, as though awaiting the wires along which they once lined the sky.

One evening not so long ago, I was standing on that little wooden bridge and saw away in the distance two columns of smoke rising from the rubble. Perhaps it was government workers continuing some interminably slow programme; or perhaps children indulging in some delinquent game. But the

27

sight of those columns against the sky put me in a melancholy mood. They were like pyres at some abandoned funeral. A graveyard, Mrs Kawakami says, and when one remembers all those people who once frequented the area, one cannot help seeing it that way.

But I am digressing. I was trying to recall here details of Setsuko's stay with us last month.

As I may have said, Setsuko spent much of the first day of her visit sitting out on the veranda, talking with her sister. At one point towards the latter part of the afternoon when my daughters were particularly deep in women's talk, I recall I left them to go in search of my grandson, who a few minutes earlier had gone running off into the house.

It was as I was coming down the corridor that a heavy thump made the whole house shake. Alarmed, I hurried on into the dining room. At that time of day, our dining room is largely in shadow, and after the brightness of the veranda, it took my eyes a moment or two to ascertain that Ichiro was not in the room at all. Then came another thump, followed by several more, together with my grandson's voice shouting: 'Yah! Yah!' The noise was coming from the adjoining piano room. I went to the doorway, listened for a moment, then quietly slid back the partition.

In contrast to the dining room, the piano room catches the sun throughout the day. It fills with a sharp, clear light, and had it been any larger, would have been an ideal place in which to take our meals. At one time, I had used it to store paintings and materials, but nowadays, apart from the upright German piano, the room is practically bare. No doubt this lack of clutter had inspired my grandson in much the same way as the veranda had earlier; for I found him progressing across the floor with a curious stamping movement, which I took to be an impersonation of someone galloping on horseback across open land. Because his back was turned to the doorway, it was some moments before he realized he was being observed.

'Oji!' he said, turning angrily. 'Can't you see I'm busy?'

'I'm sorry, Ichiro, I didn't realize.'

'I can't play with you just now!'

'I'm very sorry. But it sounded so exciting from out here I wondered if I could come in and watch.'

For a moment, my grandson went on staring at me crossly. Then he said moodily: 'All right. But you have to sit and be quiet. I'm busy.'

'Very well,' I said, with a laugh. 'Thank you very much, Ichiro.'

My grandson continued to glare at me as I crossed the room and seated myself by the window. When Ichiro had arrived with his mother the previous evening, I had made him a gift of a sketchpad and a set of coloured crayons. I now noticed the sketchpad lying on the tatami nearby, three or four of the crayons scattered around it. I could see the first few leaves of the pad had been drawn on and was about to reach over to investigate, when Ichiro suddenly recommenced the drama I had interrupted.

'Yah! Yah!'

I watched him for a while, but could make little sense of the scenes he was enacting. At intervals, he would repeat his horse movement; at other times, he appeared to be in combat with numerous invisible enemies. All the while, he continued to mutter lines of dialogue under his breath. I tried hard to make these out, but as far as I could tell he was not using actual words, simply making sounds with his tongue.

Clearly, though he did his best to ignore me, my presence was having an inhibiting effect. Several times he froze in mid-movement as though inspiration had suddenly deserted him, before throwing himself into action again. Then before long he gave up and slumped on to the floor. I wondered if I should applaud, but thought better of it.

'Very impressive, Ichiro. But tell me, who were you pretending to be?'

'You guess, Oji.'

'Hmm. Lord Yoshitsune perhaps? No? A samurai warrior, then? Hmm. Or a ninja perhaps? The Ninja of the Wind.'

'Oji's completely on the wrong scent.'

'Then tell me. Who were you?'

'Lone Ranger!'

'What?'

'Lone Ranger! Hi yo Silver!'

'Lone Ranger? Is that a cowboy?'

'Hi yo Silver!' Ichiro began to gallop again, and this time made a neighing noise.

I watched my grandson for a moment. 'How did you learn to play cowboys, Ichiro?' I asked eventually, but he just continued to gallop and neigh.

'Ichiro,' I said, more firmly, 'wait a moment and listen. It's more interesting, more interesting by far, to pretend to be someone like Lord Yoshitsune. Shall I tell you why? Ichiro, listen, Oji will explain it to you. Ichiro, listen to your Oji-san. Ichiro!'

Possibly I raised my voice more than I had intended, for he stopped and looked at me with a startled expression. I continued to look at him for a moment, then gave a sigh.

'I'm sorry, Ichiro, I shouldn't have interrupted. Of course you can be anyone you like. Even a cowboy. You must forgive your Oji-san. He was forgetting for a moment.'

My grandson continued to stare at me, and it occurred to me he was about to burst into tears or else run out of the room.

'Please, Ichiro, you just carry on with what you were doing.'

For a moment longer, Ichiro went on staring at me. Then he suddenly yelled out: 'Lone Ranger! Hi yo Silver!' and began to gallop again. He stamped more violently than ever, causing the whole room to shake around us. I went on watching him for a moment, then reached over and picked up his sketchpad.

Ichiro had used up the first four or five sheets somewhat wastefully. His technique was not at all bad, but the sketches – of trams and trains – had each been abandoned at a very early stage. Ichiro noticed me examining the sketchpad and came hurrying over.

'Oji! Who said you could look at those?' He tried to snatch the pad away from me, but I held it out of his reach.

'Now, Ichiro, don't be unkind. Oji wants to see what you've been doing with the crayons he gave you. That's only fair.' I lowered the sketchpad and opened it at the first drawing. 'Very impressive, Ichiro. Hmm. But you know, you could be even better if you wanted.'

'Oji can't see those!'

My grandson made another attempt to snatch away the pad, obliging me to hold off his hands with my arm.

'Oji! Give me back my book!'

'Now, Ichiro, stop that. Let your Oji see. Look, Ichiro, bring me those crayons over there. Bring them over and we'll draw something together. Oji will show you.'

These words had a surprising effect. My grandson immediately stopped struggling, then went to gather up the crayons scattered on the floor. When he came back, something new – a kind of fascination – had entered his manner. He seated himself beside me and held out the crayons, watching carefully, but saying nothing.

I turned the sketchpad to a new sheet and placed it on the floor in front of him. 'Let me see you do something first, Ichiro. Then Oji will see if he can help to make it better at all. What do you want to draw?'

My grandson had become very quiet. He looked down at the blank sheet thoughtfully, but made no move to start drawing.

'Why don't you try and draw something you saw yesterday?' I suggested. 'Something you saw when you first arrived in the city.'

31

Ichiro went on looking at the sketchpad. Then he looked up and asked: 'Was Oji a famous artist once?'

'A famous artist?' I gave a laugh. 'I suppose you might say that. Is that what your mother says?'

'Father says you used to be a famous artist. But you had to finish.'

'I've retired, Ichiro. Everyone retires when they get to a certain age. It's only right, they deserve a rest.'

'Father says you had to finish. Because Japan lost the war.'

I gave another laugh, then reached forward and took the sketchpad. I turned back the leaves, looking through my grandson's sketches of trams, and held one up at arm's length for a better view. 'You reach a certain age, Ichiro, and you want a rest from things. Your father too will stop working when he gets to my age. And one day, you'll be my age and you'll want a rest too. Now' – I returned to the blank sheet and placed the pad before him again – 'what will you draw for me, Ichiro?'

'Did Oji do the picture in the dining room?'

'No, that's by an artist called Urayama. Why, do you like it?'

'Did Oji paint the one in the corridor?'

'That's by another fine artist, an old friend of Oji's.'

'Where are Oji's pictures then?'

'They're tidied away for the moment. Now, Ichiro, let's get back to important things. What will you draw for me? What do you remember from yesterday? What's the matter, Ichiro? Suddenly so quiet.'

'I want to see Oji's pictures.'

'I'm sure a bright boy like you can remember all sorts of things. What about the film poster you saw? The one with the prehistoric monster. I'm sure someone like you could do it very well. Even better than the real poster perhaps.'

Ichiro seemed to consider this for a moment. Then he rolled over on to his front, and with his face close to the paper, began to draw.

Using a dark brown crayon, he drew on the lower part of the sheet a row of boxes – which soon became a skyline of city buildings. And then there emerged, looming above the city, a huge lizard-like creature up on its hind legs. At this point my grandson exchanged his brown crayon for a red one and began to make bright streaks all around the lizard.

'What is this, Ichiro? Fire?'

Ichiro continued with his red streaks, not answering.

'Why is there fire, Ichiro? Is it to do with the monster appearing?'

'Electric cables,' Ichiro said, with an impatient sigh.

'Electric cables? Now that's interesting. I wonder why electric cables cause fire. Do you know?'

Ichiro gave another sigh and continued to draw. He picked up his dark crayon again and began to draw at the foot of the sheet panic-stricken people fleeing in all directions.

'You're doing this very well, Ichiro,' I remarked. 'Perhaps as a reward, Oji might take you to see the movie tomorrow. Would you like that?'

My grandson paused and looked up. 'It might be too scary for Oji,' he said.

'I doubt that,' I said, with a laugh. 'But it may well frighten your mother and your aunt.'

At this, Ichiro burst into loud laughter. He rolled over on to his back and laughed some more. 'Mother and Aunt Noriko will be really scared!' he shouted at the ceiling.

'But we men will enjoy it, won't we, Ichiro? We'll go tomorrow. Would you like that? We'll take the women with us and watch them get frightened.'

Ichiro continued to laugh loudly. 'Aunt Noriko will get scared straightaway!'

'She probably will,' I said, laughing again myself. 'Very well, we'll all go tomorrow. Now, Ichiro, you'd better go on with your picture.'

'Aunt Noriko will get scared! She'll want to leave!'

'Now, Ichiro, let's carry on. You were doing very well.'

Ichiro rolled back over and returned to his picture. His earlier concentration, though, seemed to have deserted him; he began to add more and more fleeing figures at the bottom of his sketch until the shapes merged and became meaningless. Eventually abandoning any sense of care, he started to scribble wildly all over the lower section of the sheet.

'Ichiro, what are you doing? We won't go to the movie if you're going to do that. Ichiro, stop that!'

My grandson sprang to his feet and yelled out: 'Hi yo Silver!'

'Ichiro, sit down. You haven't finished yet.'

'Where's Aunt Noriko?'

'She's talking with your mother. Now, Ichiro, you haven't finished your picture yet. Ichiro!'

But my grandson went running out of the room, shouting: 'Lone Ranger! Hi yo Silver!'

I cannot recall precisely what I did with myself for the next several minutes. Quite possibly I remained sitting there in the piano room, gazing at Ichiro's drawings, thinking about nothing in particular as I am increasingly prone to do these days. Eventually, though, I rose to my feet and went in search of my family.

I found Setsuko sitting alone on the veranda, looking out at the garden. The sun was still bright, but the day had grown much cooler, and as I appeared Setsuko turned and moved a cushion into a patch of sunlight for me.

'We made fresh tea,' she said. 'Would you care for some, Father?'

I thanked her, and as she poured for me, I cast my gaze out to the garden.

For all it suffered during the war, our garden has recovered well, and is still recognizably the one Akira Sugimura built some forty years ago. Down at the far end, near the back wall, I could see Noriko and Ichiro examining a bamboo bush. That bush, like almost all the other shrubs and trees in the garden, had been transplanted fully grown by Sugimura from elsewhere in the city. In fact, one rumour has it that Sugimura personally walked around the city, peering over garden fences, offering large sums of money to the owner of any shrub or tree he wished to uproot for himself. If this is true, then he made his choice with admirable skill; the result was – and remains today – splendidly harmonious. There is a natural, rambling feeling about the garden, with barely a hint of artificial design.

'Noriko was always so good with children,' Setsuko remarked, her eyes on them. 'Ichiro's taken a great liking to her.'

'Ichiro's a fine boy,' I said. 'Not at all shy like a lot of children that age.'

'I hope he wasn't giving you trouble just now. He can be quite headstrong at times. Please don't hesitate to scold him if he becomes a nuisance.'

'Not at all. We're getting on fine. We were just practising some drawing together, in fact.'

'Really? I'm sure he enjoyed that.'

'He was play-acting some scenario for me too,' I said. 'He mimes his actions very well.'

'Oh yes. He occupies himself for long periods that way.'

'Does he make up his own words? I was trying to listen, but I couldn't make out what he was saying.'

My daughter raised a hand to cover her laugh. 'He must have been playing cowboys. When he plays cowboys, he tries to speak English.'

'English? Extraordinary. So that's what it was.'

'We took him once to the cinema to see an American cowboy film. He's been very fond of cowboys ever since. We even had to buy him a ten-gallon hat. He's convinced cowboys make that funny sound he does. It must have seemed very strange.'

'So that's what it was,' I said with a laugh. 'My grandson's become a cowboy.'

Down in the garden, a breeze was making the foliage sway.

Noriko was crouching down by the old stone lantern near the back wall, pointing something out to Ichiro.

'Still,' I said, with a sigh, 'only a few years ago, Ichiro wouldn't have been allowed to see such a thing as a cowboy film.'

Setsuko, without turning from the garden, said: 'Suichi believes it's better he likes cowboys than that he idolize people like Miyamoto Musashi. Suichi thinks the American heroes are the better models for children now.'

'Is that so? So that's Suichi's view.'

Ichiro seemed unimpressed by the stone lantern, for we could see him tugging violently at his aunt's arm. Beside me, Setsuko gave an embarrassed laugh.

'He's so arrogant. Pulling people back and forth. Such bad manners.'

'Incidentally,' I said, 'Ichiro and I decided we'd go to the cinema tomorrow.'

'Really?'

I could see at once the uncertainty in Setsuko's manner.

'Yes,' I said, 'he seems very keen on this prehistoric monster. Don't worry, I looked it up in the newspaper. The movie's perfectly suitable for a boy of his age.'

'Yes, I'm sure.'

'In fact, I thought we should all go. A family outing, so to speak.'

Setsuko cleared her throat nervously. 'That would be most enjoyable. Except perhaps Noriko may also have some plans for tomorrow.'

'Oh? What plans are those?'

'I believe she was wanting us all to go to the deer park. But I'm sure that can be done another time.'

'I had no idea Noriko had any plans. She certainly never asked me about them. Besides, I've already told Ichiro we'd go to the movie tomorrow. His heart will be set on it now.'

'Indeed,' said Setsuko. 'I'm sure he'd like to go to the cinema.'

Noriko was coming up the garden path towards us, Ichiro leading her by the hand. No doubt I might have taken up with her straightaway the matter of the following day, but she and Ichiro did not stay on the veranda, going inside to wash their hands. As it was, I was not able to raise the matter until after supper that evening.

Although during the day the dining room is a rather gloomy place on account of the sun rarely reaching it, after dark, with the lightshade low over the table, it has a cosy atmosphere. We had been sitting around the table for several minutes, reading newspapers and magazines, when I said to my grandson:

'Well, Ichiro, have you told your aunt about tomorrow?'

Ichiro looked up from his book with a puzzled expression.

'Shall we take the women with us or not?' I said. 'Remember what we said. They might find it too scary.'

This time my grandson understood me and grinned. 'It might be too scary for Aunt Noriko,' he said. 'Do you want to come, Aunt Noriko?'

'Come to what, Ichiro-san?' Noriko asked.

'Monster film.'

'I thought we would all go tomorrow to the cinema,' I explained. 'A family outing, so to speak.'

'Tomorrow?' Noriko looked at me, then turned to my grandson. 'Well, we can't go tomorrow, can we, Ichiro? We're going to the deer park, remember?'

'The deer park can wait,' I said. 'The boy's looking forward to his film now.'

'Nonsense,' Noriko said. 'Everything's arranged. We're going to call in on Mrs Watanabe on the way back. She's been wanting to meet Ichiro. Anyway, we decided a long time ago. Didn't we, Ichiro?'

'It's very kind of Father,' Setsuko put in. 'But I understand Mrs Watanabe is expecting us. Perhaps we should leave the cinema until the day after.'

'But Ichiro's been looking forward to it,' I protested. 'Isn't that so, Ichiro? What a nuisance these women are.'

Ichiro did not look at me, apparently absorbed again in his book.

'You tell these women, Ichiro,' I said.

My grandson continued to stare at his book.

'Ichiro.'

Suddenly, dropping his book on the table, he got to his feet and went running out of the room, through into the piano room.

I gave a small laugh. 'There,' I said to Noriko. 'You've disappointed him now. You should have left things as they were.'

'Don't be ridiculous, Father. We'd arranged Mrs Watanabe's long ago. Besides, it's ridiculous to take Ichiro to see a film like that. He won't enjoy a film like that, will he, Setsuko?'

My elder daughter smiled uncomfortably. 'It's very kind of Father,' she said, quietly. 'Perhaps the day after . . .'

I gave a sigh, shaking my head, and returned to my newspaper. But when after a few minutes it became clear that neither of my daughters was going to bring Ichiro back, I got up myself and went into the piano room.

Ichiro, unable to reach the cord on the lightshade, had switched on the lamp on top of the piano. I found him sitting on the piano stool, one side of his head resting on the piano lid. His features, squashed against the dark wood, bore a disgruntled look.

'I'm sorry about this, Ichiro,' I said. 'But don't be disappointed. We'll go the day after.'

Ichiro gave no reaction, so I said: 'Now, Ichiro, this is nothing to be so disappointed about.'

I walked over to the window. It had become quite dark outside, and all I could see was my reflection and that of the room behind me. From the other room, I could hear the women talking in lowered voices.

'Cheer up, Ichiro,' I said. 'This is nothing to get upset about. We'll go the day after, I promise you.'

When I turned again to Ichiro, his head was resting on the piano lid as before; but now, he was walking his fingers along the lid, as though playing the keys.

I gave a light laugh. 'Well, Ichiro, we'll just go the day after. We can't have the women ruling over us, can we?' I gave another laugh. 'I expect they thought it would be too scary. Eh, Ichiro?'

My grandson still gave no response, though he continued his finger movements on the piano lid. I decided it would be best to leave him alone for a few moments, and giving another laugh, went back through into the dining room.

I found my daughters sitting in silence, reading their magazines. As I sat down, I gave a heavy sigh, but neither of them responded to this. I had replaced my reading glasses on my face and was about to start on my newspaper, when Noriko said in a quiet voice: 'Father, shall we make some tea?'

'That's kind of you, Noriko. But not for me just now.'

'What about you, Setsuko?'

'Thank you, Noriko. But I don't think I will either.'

We continued to read in silence for a few more moments. Then Setsuko said: 'Will Father be coming with us tomorrow? We could still have our family outing then.'

'I'd like to. But I'm afraid there're a few things I have to be getting on with tomorrow.'

'What do you mean?' Noriko broke in. 'What things are those?' Then turning to Setsuko, she said: 'Don't listen to Father. He's got nothing to do these days. He'll just mope about the house like he always does now.'

'It would be very pleasant if Father would accompany us,' Setsuko said to me.

'It's regrettable,' I said, looking down at my newspaper again. 'But I have one or two things to attend to.'

'So you're going to stay at home all on your own?' Noriko asked.

'If you're all going away, it seems I'll have to.'

Setsuko gave a polite cough. Then she said: 'Perhaps then I'll remain at home also. Father and I have had little chance to exchange news.'

Noriko stared across the table at her sister. 'There's no need for you to miss out. You've come all this way, you don't want to spend all your time indoors.'

'But I would very much enjoy staying and keeping Father company. I expect we have a lot more news to exchange.'

'Father, look what you've done,' Noriko said. Then to her sister, she said: 'So it's only me and Ichiro now.'

'Ichiro will enjoy spending the day with you, Noriko,' Setsuko said with a smile. 'You're very much his favourite at the moment.'

I was glad about Setsuko's decision to remain at home, for indeed, we had had little opportunity to talk without interruption; and there are, of course, many things a father wishes to know about a married daughter's life which he cannot ask outright. But what never occurred to me that evening was that Setsuko would have her own reasons for wishing to remain in the house with me.

It is perhaps a sign of my advancing years that I have taken to wandering into rooms for no purpose. When Setsuko slid open the door of the reception room that afternoon – on the second day of her visit – I must have been standing there lost in thought for some considerable time.

'I'm sorry,' she said. 'I'll come back later.'

I turned, a little startled, to find my daughter kneeling at the threshold, holding a vase filled with flowers and cuttings.

'No, please come in,' I said to her. 'I was doing nothing in particular.'

Retirement places more time on your hands. Indeed, it is one of the enjoyments of retirement that you are able to drift through the day at your own pace, easy in the knowledge that you have put hard work and achievement behind you. Nevertheless, I must be getting absent-minded indeed to be wandering aimlessly into – of all places – the reception room. For thoughout my years I have preserved the sense, instilled in me by my father, that the reception room of a house is a place to be revered, a place to be kept unsoiled by everyday trivialities, reserved for the receiving of important guests, or else the paying of respects at the Buddhist altar. Accordingly, the reception room of my house has always had a more solemn atmosphere than that to be found in most households; and although I never made a rule of it as my own father did, I discouraged my children while they were young from entering the room unless specifically bidden to do so.

My respect for reception rooms may well appear exaggerated, but then you must realize that in the house I grew up in – in Tsuruoka Village, a half-day's train journey from here – I was forbidden even to enter the reception room until the age of twelve. That room being in many senses the centre of the house, curiosity compelled me to construct an image of its interior from the occasional glimpses I managed to catch of it. Later in my life I was often to surprise colleagues with my ability to realize a scene on canvas based only on the briefest of passing glances; it is possible I have my father to thank for this skill, and the inadvertent training he gave my artist's eye during those formative years. In any case, when I reached the age of twelve, the 'business meetings' began, and then I found myself inside that room once every week.

'Masuji and I will be discussing business tonight,' my father would announce during supper. And that would serve both as my summons to present myself after the meal, and as a warning to the rest of the family to make no noise in the vicinity of the reception room that evening.

My father would disappear into the room after supper, and call me some fifteen minutes later. The room I entered would be lit by a single tall candle standing in the centre of the floor. Within the circle of light it cast, my father would be sitting cross-legged on the tatami before his wooden 'business box'. He would gesture for me to sit opposite him in the light, and as I did so, the brightness of the candle would put the rest of the room into shadow. Only vaguely would I be able to discern past my father's shoulder the Buddhist altar by the far wall, or the few hangings adorning the alcoves.

My father would then begin his talking. From out of his 'business box' he would produce small, fat notebooks, some of which he would open so that he could point out to me columns of densely packed figures. All the while, his talking would continue in a measured, grave tone, to pause only occasionally when he would look up at me as though for confirmation. At these points, I would hurriedly utter: 'Yes, indeed.'

Of course, it was quite impossible for me to follow what my father was saying. Employing jargon, recounting his way through lengthy calculations, he made no concessions to the fact that he was addressing a young boy. But it seemed equally impossible for me to ask him to stop and explain. For as I saw it, I had been allowed into the reception room only because I had been deemed old enough to understand such talk. My sense of shame was matched only by a terrible fear that at any moment I would be called upon to say more than 'Yes, indeed' and my game would be up. And although month after month went by and I was never required to say anything more, I nevertheless lived in dread of the next 'business meeting'.

Of course, it is clear to me now that my father never expected me for a moment to follow his talk, but I have never ascertained just why he put me through these ordeals. Perhaps he wished to impress upon me from that early age his expectation that I would eventually take over the family business. Or perhaps he felt that as future head of the family, it was only right I should be consulted on all decisions whose repercussions were likely to extend into my adulthood; that way, so my father may have figured it, I would have less cause for complaint were I to inherit an unsound business.

Then when I was fifteen, I remember being called into the reception room for a different kind of meeting. As ever, the room was lit by the tall candle, my father sat at the centre of its light. But that evening, instead of his business box, he had before him a heavy earthenware ashpot. This puzzled me, for this ashpot – the largest in the house – was normally produced only for guests.

'You've brought all of them?' he asked.

'I've done as you instructed.'

I laid beside my father the pile of paintings and sketches I had been holding in my arms. They made an untidy pile, sheets of varying sizes and quality, most of which had warped or wrinkled with the paint.

I sat in silence while my father looked through my work. He would regard each painting for a moment, then lay it to one side. When he was almost half-way through my collection, he said without looking up:

'Masuji, are you sure all your work is here? Aren't there one or two paintings you haven't brought me?'

I did not answer immediately. He looked up and asked: 'Well?'

'It's possible there may be one or two I have not brought.'

'Indeed. And no doubt, Masuji, the missing paintings are the very ones you're most proud of. Isn't that so?'

He had turned his eyes down to the paintings again, so I did not answer. For several more moments, I watched him going through the pile. Once, he held one painting close to the candle flame, saying: 'This is the path leading down from Nishiyama hill, is it not? Certainly you've caught the likeness very well. That's just how it looks coming down the hill. Very skilful.'

'Thank you.'

'You know, Masuji' – my father's eyes were still fixed on the painting – 'I've heard a curious thing from your mother. She seems to be under the impression you wish to take up painting as a profession.'

He did not phrase this as a question, so I did not at first reply. But then he looked up and repeated: 'Your mother, Masuji, seems to be under the impression that you wish to take up painting as a profession. Naturally, she is mistaken in supposing this.'

'Naturally,' I said, quietly.

'You mean, there has been some misunderstanding on her part.'

'No doubt.'

'I see.'

For a few more minutes, my father continued to study the paintings, and I sat there watching him in silence. Then he said without looking up: 'In fact, I think that was your mother going by outside. Did you hear her?'

'I'm afraid I didn't hear anyone.'

'I think it was your mother. Ask her to step in here since she's passing.'

I rose to my feet and went to the doorway. The corridor was dark and empty, as I had known it would be. Behind me, I heard my father's voice say: 'While you're fetching her, Masuji, gather together the rest of your paintings and bring them to me.'

Perhaps it was simply my imagination, but when I returned to the room a few minutes later, accompanied by my mother, I received the impression the earthenware ashpot had been moved slightly nearer the candle. I also thought there was a smell of burning in the air, but when I glanced into the ashpot, there were no signs of its having been used.

My father acknowledged me distractedly when I placed the last examples of my work beside the original pile. He appeared still to be preoccupied with my paintings, and for some time, he ignored both my mother and me, seated before him in silence. Then finally, he gave a sigh, looked up and said to me: 'I don't expect, Masuji, you have much time for wandering priests, do you?'

'Wandering priests? I suppose not.'

'They have a lot to say about this world. I don't pay much attention to them most of the time. But it's only decent to be courteous to holy men, even if they strike you sometimes as nothing more than beggars.'

He paused, so I said: 'Yes, indeed.'

Then my father turned to my mother and said: 'Do you remember, Sachiko, the wandering priests who used to come through this village? There was one who came to this house just after our son here was born. A thin old man, with only one hand. But a very sturdy fellow for all that. You remember him?'

'Yes, of course,' my mother said. 'But perhaps one should not take to heart what some of these priests have to say.'

'But you remember,' my father said, 'this priest gained a deep insight into Masuji's heart. He left us with a warning, you remember, Sachiko?'

'But our son was no more than a baby then,' my mother said. Her voice was lowered, as though she somehow hoped I would not hear. In contrast, my father's voice was needlessly loud, as if addressing an audience:

'He left us with a warning. Masuji's limbs were healthy, he told us, but he had been born with a flaw in his nature. A weak streak that would give him a tendency towards slothfulness and deceit. You remember this, Sachiko?'

'But I believe the priest also had many positive things to say about our son.'

'This is true. Our son had a lot of good qualities, the priest did point that out. But you recall his warning, Sachiko? He said if the good points were to dominate, we who brought him up would have to be vigilant and check this weak streak whenever it tried to manifest itself. Otherwise, so the old priest told us, Masuji here would grow up to be a good-for-nothing.'

'But perhaps,' my mother said cautiously, 'it is unwise to take to heart what these priests have to say.'

My father appeared a little surprised by this remark. Then,

after a moment, he nodded thoughtfully, as though my mother had made a perplexing point. 'I was myself reluctant to take him seriously at the time,' he continued. 'But then at every stage of Masuji's growing up, I've been obliged to acknowledge that old man's words. It can't be denied, there is a weakness running through our son's character. There's little in the way of malice in him. But unceasingly, we've had to combat his laziness, his dislike of useful work, his weak will.'

Then, with some deliberation, my father picked up three or four of my paintings and held them in both hands as though to test their weight. He turned his gaze towards me and said: 'Masuji, your mother here was under the impression that you wished to pursue painting as a profession. Has there perhaps been some misunderstanding on her part?'

I lowered my eyes and remained silent. Then I heard my mother's voice beside me, almost whispering, say: 'He's still very young. I'm sure it's just a childish whim of his.'

There was a pause, then my father said: 'Tell me, Masuji, have you any idea what kind of a world artists inhabit?'

I remained silent, looking at the floor before me.

'Artists', my father's voice continued, 'live in squalor and poverty. They inhabit a world which gives them every temptation to become weak-willed and depraved. Am I not right, Sachiko?'

'Naturally. Yet perhaps there are one or two who are able to pursue an artistic career and yet avoid such pitfalls.'

'Of course, there are exceptions,' my father said. My eyes were still lowered, but I could tell from his voice that he was again nodding in his perplexed manner. 'The handful with extraordinary resolve and character. But I'm afraid our son here is far from being such a person. Indeed, quite the contrary. It is our duty to protect him from such dangers. We do, after all, wish him to become someone we can be proud of, don't we?'

'Of course,' my mother said.

I looked up quickly. The candle had burned half-way down

its length and the flame was sharply illuminating one side of my father's face. He had now placed the paintings on his lap, and I noticed how his fingers were moving impatiently along their edges.

'Masuji,' he said, 'you may leave us now. I wish to speak with your mother.'

I can remember a little later that night, coming across my mother in the darkness. In all likelihood, it was in one of the corridors that I encountered her, though I do not remember this. Neither do I remember why I was wandering around the house in the dark, but it was certainly not in order to eavesdrop on my parents – for I do recall being resolved to pay no heed to what occurred in the reception room after my departure. In those days, of course, houses were all badly lit, so it was not at all unusual that we should stand in the dark and converse. I could make out my mother's figure in front of me, but could not see her face.

'There's a smell of burning around the house,' I remarked.

'Burning?' My mother was silent for a while, then she said: 'No. I don't think so. It must be your imagination, Masuji.'

'I smelt burning,' I said. 'There, I just caught it again. Is Father still in the reception room?'

'Yes. He's working on something.'

'Whatever he's doing in there,' I said, 'it doesn't bother me in the least.'

My mother made no sound, so I added: 'The only thing Father's succeeded in kindling is my ambition.'

'That is good to hear, Masuji.'

'You mustn't misunderstand me, Mother. I have no wish to find myself in years to come, sitting where Father is now sitting, telling my own son about accounts and money. Would you be proud of me if I grew to be like that?'

'I would indeed, Masuji. There is much more to a life like your father's than you can possibly know at your age.'

'I would never be proud of myself. When I said I was ambitious, I meant I wished to rise above such a life.'

My mother fell silent for some moments. Then she said: 'When you are young, there are many things which appear dull and lifeless. But as you get older, you will find these are the very things that are most important to you.'

I did not reply to this. Instead, I believe I said: 'Once, I was terrified of Father's business meetings. But for some time now, they've simply bored me. In fact, they disgust me. What are these meetings I'm so privileged to attend? The counting of loose change. The fingering of coins, hour after hour. I would never forgive myself if my life came to be like that.' I paused and waited to see if my mother would say anything. For a moment, I had a peculiar feeling she had walked silently away while I had been speaking and I was now standing there alone. But then I heard her move just in front of me, so I repeated: 'It doesn't bother me in the least what Father's doing in the reception room. All he's kindled is my ambition.'

However, I see I am drifting. My intention had been to record here that conversation I had with Setsuko last month when she came into the reception room to change the flowers.

As I recall it, Setsuko had seated herself before the Buddhist altar and had begun to remove the more tired of the flowers decorating it. I had seated myself a little behind her, watching the way she carefully shook each stem before placing it on her lap, and I believe we were talking about something quite light-hearted at that stage. But then she said, without turning from her flowers:

'Excuse me for mentioning this, Father. No doubt, it would have already occurred to you.'

'What is that, Setsuko?'

'I merely mention it because I gather it is very likely Noriko's marriage negotiations will progress.'

Setsuko had begun to transfer, one by one, the fresh cuttings from out of her vase into those surrounding the altar. She was performing this task with great care, pausing after each flower to consider the effect. 'I merely wished to say,' she went on, 'once the negotiations begin in earnest, it may be as well if Father were to take certain precautionary steps.'

'Precautionary steps? Naturally, we'll go carefully. But what precisely did you have in mind?'

'Forgive me, I was referring particularly to the investigations.'

'Well, of course, we'll be as thorough as necessary. We'll hire the same detective as last year. He was very reliable, you may remember.'

Setsuko carefully repositioned a stem. 'Forgive me, I am no doubt expressing myself unclearly. I was, in fact, referring to *their* investigations.'

'I'm sorry, I'm not sure I follow you. I was not aware we had anything to hide.'

Setsuko gave a nervous laugh. 'Father must forgive me. As you know, I've never had a gift for conversation. Suichi is forever scolding me for expressing myself badly. He expresses himself so eloquently. No doubt, I should endeavour to learn from him.'

'I'm sure your conversation is fine, but I'm afraid I don't quite follow what you are saying.'

Suddenly, Setsuko raised her hands in despair. 'The breeze,' she said with a sigh, and reached forward to her flowers once more. 'I like them like this, but the breeze doesn't seem to agree.' For a moment, she became pre-occupied again. Then she said: 'You must forgive me, Father. In my place, Suichi would express things better. But of course, he isn't here. I merely wished to say that it is perhaps wise if Father would take certain precautionary steps. To ensure misunderstandings do not arise. After all, Noriko is almost twenty-six now. We cannot afford many more disappointments such as last year's.'

'Misunderstandings about what, Setsuko?'

'About the past. But please, I'm sure I'm speaking quite needlessly. Father has no doubt thought already of all these things and will do whatever is necessary.'

She sat back, pondering her work, then turned to me with a

smile. 'I have little skill in these things,' she said, indicating the flowers.

'They look splendid.'

She gave a doubtful glance towards the altar and laughed self-consciously.

Yesterday, as I was enjoying the tram ride down to the quiet suburb of Arakawa, the recollection of that exchange in the reception room came into my mind, causing me to experience a wave of irritation. As I looked out of the window at the scenery, growing ever less cluttered as we continued south, the image returned to my mind of my daughter seated in front of the altar, advising me to take 'precautionary steps'. I remembered again the way she had turned her face towards me slightly to say: 'After all, we cannot afford many more disappointments such as last year's.' And I remembered again her knowing manner on the veranda that first morning of her visit, when she had hinted I had some peculiar secret about the Miyakes' withdrawal last year. Such recollections had already marred my mood over this past month; but it was yesterday, in the tranquillity of travelling alone to the quieter reaches of the city, that I was able to consider my feelings more clearly, and I came to realize my sense of irritation was not essentially directed against Setsuko, but against her husband.

It is, I suppose, natural enough that a wife is influenced by her husband's ideas – even, as in the case of Suichi's, when they are quite irrational. But when a man induces his wife to turn suspicious thoughts against her own father, then that is surely cause enough for resentment. On account of what he must have suffered out in Manchuria, I have in the past tried to adopt a tolerant attitude towards certain aspects of his behaviour; I have not taken personally, for instance, the frequent signs of bitterness he has displayed towards my generation. But then I always assumed such feelings fade with time. However, so far as Suichi is concerned, they seem to be actually growing more trenchant and unreasonable.

All this would not be bothering me now – after all, Setsuko and Suichi live far away, and I never see them more than once a year – if it were not that latterly, ever since Setsuko's visit last month, these same irrational ideas seem to be infecting Noriko's mind. This is what has irritated me and tempted me several times these past few days to write an angry letter to Setsuko. It is all very well a husband and wife occupying each other with ridiculous speculations, but they should keep such things to themselves. A stricter father, no doubt, would have done something long ago.

More than once last month, I had come upon my daughters deep in discussion and noticed how they broke off guiltily before starting some fresh, rather unconvincing conversation. In fact, I can recall this happening at least three times during the course of the five days Setsuko spent here. And then just a few days ago, Noriko and I were finishing breakfast when she said to me:

'I was walking past the Shimizu department store yesterday and guess who I saw standing at the tram stop? It was Jiro Miyake!'

'Miyake?' I looked up from my bowl, surprised to hear Noriko mentioning the name so brazenly. 'Why, that was unfortunate.'

'Unfortunate? Well actually, Father, I was rather pleased to see him. He seemed embarrassed though, so I didn't talk to him for long. In any case, I had to get back to the office. I was just out on an errand, you see. But did you know he's engaged to be married now?'

'He told you that? What a nerve.'

'He didn't volunteer it, of course. I asked him. I told him I was in the middle of new negotiations now and asked him how his own marriage prospects were. I asked him just like that. His face was going scarlet! But then he came out with it and said he was all but engaged now. It's all practically settled.'

'Really, Noriko, you shouldn't be so indiscreet. Why did you have to mention marriage at all?'

'I was curious. I'm not upset about it any more. And with the present negotiations going so well, I was just thinking the other day, what a pity it would be if Jiro Miyake was still brooding over last year. So you can imagine how pleased I was to find him practically engaged.'

'I see.'

'I hope I get to meet his bride soon. I'm sure she's very nice, aren't you, Father?'

'I'm sure.'

We continued eating for a moment. Then Noriko said: 'There was something else I almost asked him. But I didn't.' She leaned forward and whispered: 'I almost asked about last year. About why they pulled out.'

'It's just as well you didn't. Besides, they gave their reason clearly enough at the time. They felt the young man was inadequately placed to be worthy of you.'

'But you know that was just formality, Father. We never found out the real reason. At least, I never got to hear about it.' It was at this point that something in her voice made me look up again from my bowl. Noriko was holding her chopsticks poised in the air, as though waiting for me to say something. Then, as I continued eating, she said: 'Why do you suppose they pulled out? Did you ever discover about that?'

'I discovered nothing. As I say, they said they felt the young man was inadequately placed. It's a perfectly good answer.'

'I wonder, Father, if it was simply that I didn't come up to their requirements. Perhaps I wasn't pretty enough. Do you think that's what it was?'

'It wasn't anything to do with you, you know that. There are all sorts of reasons why a family pulls out of a negotiation.'

'Well, Father, if it wasn't to do with me, then I wonder what it could have been to make them pull out like that.'

It seemed to me there was something unnaturally deliberate in the way my daughter uttered those words. Perhaps I imagined it, but then a father comes to notice any small inflexions in his daughter's speech.

In any case, that exchange with Noriko put me in mind again of the occasion I myself had encountered Jiro Miyake and had ended up talking with him at a tram stop. It was just over a year ago – the negotiations with the Miyake family were still going on at that point – towards the late afternoon when the city was full of people returning home after the day's work. For some reason, I had been walking through the Yokote district and was making towards the tram stop outside the Kimura Company Building. If you are familiar with the Yokote district, you will know of the numerous small, rather seedy offices that line the upper storeys of the shops there. When I encountered Jiro Miyake that day, he was emerging from one such office, having come down a narrow staircase between two shop fronts.

I had met him twice prior to that day, but only at formal family meetings when he had turned out in his best clothes. Now he looked quite different, dressed in a tired-looking raincoat a little too large for him, clutching a briefcase under his arm. He had the appearance of a young man much accustomed to being bossed around; indeed, his whole posture seemed to be fixed on the verge of bowing. When I asked him if the office he had just left was his workplace, he began laughing nervously, as though I had caught him coming out of some disreputable house.

It did occur to me his awkwardness was perhaps too extreme to be accounted for merely by our chance meeting; but at the time I put it down to his embarrassment at the shabby appearance of his office building and its surroundings. It was only a week or so afterwards, when learning with surprise that the Miyakes had pulled out, that I found myself casting my mind back to that encounter, searching it for significance.

'I wonder,' I said to Setsuko, for she was down on one of her visits at the time, 'if all the while I was talking with him, they'd already decided on a withdrawal.'

'That would certainly account for the nervousness Father observed,' Setsuko had said. 'Did he not say anything to hint at their intentions?'

But even then, only a week after the actual encounter, I could hardly recall the conversation I had had with young Miyake. That afternoon, of course, I was still going on the assumption that his engagement to Noriko would be announced any day, and that I was dealing with a future member of my family. My attentions, then, were focused on getting young Miyake to relax in my presence, and I did not give as much thought as I might to what was actually said during our short walk to the tram stop and the few minutes we spent standing there together.

Nevertheless, as I pondered over the whole business during the days which followed, a new idea struck me: that perhaps the encounter itself had helped bring about the withdrawal.

'It's just possible,' I put it to Setsuko. 'Miyake was very self-conscious about my having seen his workplace. Possibly it struck him afresh that there was too much of a gulf between our families. After all, it's a point they've made too often for it to be just formality.'

But Setsuko, it would seem, was unconvinced by that theory. And it seems she must have gone home to her husband to speculate over the failure of her sister's proposal. For this year, she appears to have returned with her own theories – or at least, those of Suichi. So then I am obliged to think back yet again to that encounter with Miyake, to turn it over from yet another perspective. But as I have said, I could barely recall what had taken place just one week afterwards, and now more than a year has passed.

But then one particular exchange has come back to me which I gave little significance to before. Miyake and I had reached the main street and were standing in front of the Kimura Company Building awaiting our respective trams. And I remember Miyake saying:

'We had some sad news at work today. The President of our parent company is now deceased.'

'I'm very sorry to hear that. Was he advanced in years?'

'He was only in his early sixties. I never had the chance to see him in the flesh, though of course I saw photographs of him in our periodicals. He was a great man, and we all feel as though we've been orphaned.'

'It must be a blow to you all.'

'Indeed it is,' Miyake said, and paused for a moment. Then he continued: 'However, we at our office are at something of a loss as to the most appropriate way of showing our respect. You see, to be quite frank, the President committed suicide.'

'Really?'

'Indeed. He was found gassed. But it seems he tried hara-kiri first, for there were minor scratches around his stomach.' Miyake looked down at the ground solemnly. 'It was his apology on behalf of the companies under his charge.'

'His apology?'

'Our President clearly felt responsible for certain undertakings we were involved in during the war. Two senior men were already dismissed by the Americans, but our President obviously felt it was not enough. His act was an apology on behalf of us all to the families of those killed in the war.'

'Why, really,' I said, 'that seems rather extreme. The world seems to have gone mad. Every day there seems to be a report of someone else killing himself in apology. Tell me, Mr Miyake, don't you find it all a great waste? After all, if your country is at war, you do all you can in support, there's no shame in that. What need is there to apologize by death?'

'No doubt you're right, sir. But to be frank, there's much relief around the company. We feel now we can forget our past transgressions and look to the future. It was a great thing our President did.'

'But a great waste, too. Some of our best men are giving up their lives in this way.'

'Indeed, sir, it is a pity. Sometimes I think there are many who should be giving their lives in apology who are too cowardly to face up to their responsibilities. It is then left to the likes of our President to carry out the noble gestures. There are plenty of men already back in positions they held during the war. Some of them are no better than war criminals. They should be the ones apologizing.'

'I see your point,' I said. 'But those who fought and worked loyally for our country during the war cannot be called war criminals. I fear that's an expression used too freely these days.'

'But these are the men who led the country astray, sir. Surely, it's only right they should acknowledge their responsibility. It's a cowardice that these men refuse to admit to their mistakes. And when those mistakes were made on behalf of the whole country, why then it must be the greatest cowardice of all.'

Did Miyake really say all this to me that afternoon? Perhaps I am getting his words confused with the sort of thing Suichi will come out and say. This is quite possible; I had after all come to regard Miyake as my prospective son-in-law, and I may indeed have somehow associated him with my actual son-in-law. Certainly, phrases like 'the greatest cowardice of all' sound much more like Suichi than the mild-mannered young Miyake. I am certain enough, though, that some such conversation did take place at the tram stop that day, and I suppose it is somewhat curious he should have brought up such a topic as he did. But as for the phrase 'the greatest cowardice of all', I am sure that is Suichi's. In fact, now I think of it, I am sure Suichi used it that evening after the ceremony for the burying of Kenji's ashes.

It had taken more than a year for my son's ashes to arrive from Manchuria. The communists, we were constantly told, had made everything difficult there. Then when his ashes finally came, along with those of the twenty-three other young men who had died attempting that hopeless charge across the minefield, there were no assurances the ashes were in fact Kenji's and Kenji's alone. 'But if my brother's ashes are mingled,' Setsuko had written to me at the time, 'they would only be mingled with those of his comrades. We cannot complain about that.' And so we accepted the ashes as Kenji's and carried out the belated ceremony for him two years ago last month.

It was in the midst of the ceremony at the cemetery that I saw Suichi striding away angrily. When I asked Setsuko what the matter was with her husband, she whispered quickly: 'Please forgive him, he isn't well. A touch of malnutrition, he hasn't shaken it off for months.'

But later, as the guests from the ceremony were gathering in my house, Setsuko said to me: 'Please understand, Father. Such ceremonies upset Suichi deeply.'

'How touching,' I said. 'I had no idea he was so close to your brother.'

'They got on well whenever they met,' Setsuko said. 'Besides, Suichi identifies very much with the likes of Kenji. He says it could so easily have been him.'

'But isn't that all the more reason not to desert the ceremony?'

'I'm sorry, Father, Suichi never intended to appear disrespectful. But we have attended so many such ceremonies this past year, for Suichi's friends and comrades, and they always make him so angry.'

'Angry? What is it he's angry about?'

But more guests were arriving at that point and I was obliged to break off our conversation. It was not until later that evening I got a chance to talk to Suichi himself. Many of the guests were still with us, gathered in the reception room. I spotted my son-in-law's tall figure across the room, standing alone; he had parted the screens which opened on to the garden, and with his back turned to the hum of conversation, was gazing out into the darkness. I went up to him and said:

'Setsuko tells me, Suichi, these ceremonies make you angry.'

He turned and smiled. 'I suppose they do. I get angry thinking about things. About the waste.'

'Yes. It's terrible to think of the waste. But Kenji, like many others, died very bravely.'

For a moment, my son-in-law gazed at me with a still, expressionless face; it is something he does from time to time which I have never quite got used to. The gaze, no doubt, is quite innocent, but perhaps because Suichi is a physically powerful man and his features rather fearsome, it is easy to read something threatening or accusing there.

'There seems to be no end of courageous deaths,' he said, eventually. 'Half of my high school graduation year have died courageous deaths. They were all for stupid causes, though they were never to know that. Do you know, Father, what really makes me angry?'

'What is that, Suichi?'

'Those who sent the likes of Kenji out there to die these brave deaths, where are they today? They're carrying on with their lives, much the same as ever. Many are more successful than before, behaving so well in front of the Americans, the very ones who led us to disaster. And yet it's the likes of Kenji we have to mourn. This is what makes me angry. Brave young men die for stupid causes, and the real culprits are still with us. Afraid to show themselves for what they are, to admit their responsibility.' And it was then, I am sure, as he turned back to the darkness outside, that he said: 'To my mind, that's the greatest cowardice of all.'

I had been drained by the ceremony, otherwise I might have challenged some of his assumptions. But I judged there would be other opportunities for such talk and moved the conversation to other matters. I recall standing there with him, looking out into the night, enquiring about his work and about Ichiro. At that point, I had hardly seen Suichi since his return from the war, and that was my first experience of the changed, somewhat bitter son-in-law I have now come to get used to. I was surprised that evening to find him talking in that way, with no trace of the rigid manners he had had before going to war; but I put it down to the emotional effect of the burial ceremony, and more generally, to the enormous impact of his war experience – which, so Setsuko had hinted, had been of a terrible nature.

But in fact the mood I found him in that evening proved to be typical of his general mood these days; the transformation from the polite, self-effacing young man who married Setsuko two years before the war is quite remarkable. Of course, it is tragic that so many of his generation died as they did, but why must he harbour such bitterness for his elders? There is a hardness, almost a maliciousness to Suichi's views now which I find worrying – even more so since they appear to be influencing Setsuko.

But such a transformation is by no means unique to my son-in-law. These days I see it all around me; something has changed in the character of the younger generation in a way I do not fully understand, and certain aspects of this change are undeniably disturbing. For instance, just the other night down at Mrs Kawakami's, I overheard a man sitting further along the counter saying:

'I hear they took that idiot to hospital. A few broken ribs and concussion.'

'You mean the Hirayama boy?' Mrs Kawakami asked, with a look of concern.

'Is that his name? The one's who's always wandering around shouting things out. Someone really ought to get him to stop. It seems he got beaten up again last night. It's a shame, taking on an idiot like that, whatever he's shouting out.'

At this point, I turned to the man and said: 'Excuse me, you say the Hirayama boy's been attacked? For what reason?'

'It seems he kept singing one of those old military songs and chanting regressive slogans.'

'But the Hirayama boy's always done that,' I pointed out. 'He's only able to sing two or three songs. It's what he was taught.'

The man shrugged. 'I agree, what's the sense in beating up an idiot like that? It's just callousness. But he was over by the Kayabashi bridge, and you know how sleazy things get there after dark. He'd been sitting up on the bridge post, singing and chanting for about an hour. They could hear him in the bar across the way, and it seems a few of them got tired of it.'

'What sense is there in that?' Mrs Kawakami said. 'The Hirayama boy means no harm.'

'Well, someone should teach him to sing new songs,' the man said, drinking from his glass. 'He'll only get beaten up again if he goes around singing those old ones.'

We still call him 'the Hirayama boy' though he must now be at least fifty. But then the name does not seem inappropriate, for he has the mental age of a child. As far back as I can remember, he has been looked after by the Catholic nuns at the mission, but presumably he was born into a family called Hirayama. In the old days, when our pleasure district was flourishing, the Hirayama boy could always be found sitting on the ground near the entrance to the Migi-Hidari or one of its neighbouring establishments. He was, as Mrs Kawakami had said, quite harmless, and indeed, in the years before and during the war he became a popular figure in the pleasure district with his war songs and mimicking of patriotic speeches.

Who had taught him his songs, I do not know. There were no more than two or three in his repertoire, and he knew only a verse of each. But he would deliver these in a voice of considerable carrying power, and between the singing, he would amuse spectators by standing there grinning at the sky, his hands on his hips, shouting: 'This village must provide its share of sacrifices for the Emperor! Some of you will lay down your lives! Some of you will return triumphant to a new dawn!' – or some such words. And people would say,

'The Hirayama boy may not have it all there, but he's got the right attitude. He's Japanese.' I often saw people stop to give him money, or else buy him something to eat, and on those occasions the idiot's face would light up into a smile. No doubt, the Hirayama boy became fixated on those patriotic songs because of the attention and popularity they earned him.

Nobody minded idiots in those days. What has come over people that they feel inclined to beat the man up? They may not like his songs and speeches, but in all likelihood they are the same people who once patted his head and encouraged him until those few snatches embedded themselves in his brain.

But as I say, there is a different mood in the country these days, and Suichi's attitudes are probably by no means exceptional. Perhaps I am being unfair if I credit young Miyake, too, with such bitterness, but then the way things are at present, if you examine anything anyone says to you, it seems you will find a thread of this same bitter feeling running through it. For all I know, Miyake did speak those words; perhaps all men of Miyake's and Suichi's generation have come to think and speak like that.

I believe I have already mentioned that yesterday I took a trip down to the south of the city, to the Arakawa district. Arakawa is the last stop on the city tramline going south, and many people express surprise that the line should extend so far down into the suburbs. Indeed, it is hard to think of Arakawa, with its cleanly swept residential streets, its rows of maple trees on the pavements, its dignified houses each set apart from the next, and its general air of being surrounded by countryside, as being part of the city. But to my mind, the authorities were correct to take the tramline as far as Arakawa; it can only be of benefit to city-dwellers that they have easy access to calmer, less crowded surroundings. We were not always so well served, and I can recall how the hemmed-in feeling one gets in a city, especially during the hot summer weeks, was significantly greater in the days before the present tramlines were laid down.

I believe it was 1931 when the present lines began to operate, superseding the inadequate lines which had so irritated passengers for the previous thirty years. If you were not living here then, it is perhaps hard to imagine the impact these new lines had on many aspects of life in the city. Whole districts seemed to change character overnight; parks that had always been busy with people became deserted; long-established businesses suffered severe losses.

There were, of course, those districts which found themselves unexpectedly benefited, and among these was that area on the other side of the Bridge of Hesitation soon to become our pleasure district. Prior to the new tramlines, you would have found there only a few dull back streets with rows of shingled-roof houses. No one at that time considered it a district in its own right and one could only locate it by saying 'east of Furukawa'. The new tram circuit, however, meant that passengers disembarking at the terminus in Furukawa could reach the city centre more quickly on foot than by making a second, highly circuitous tram journey, and the result was a sudden influx of people walking through that area. The handful of bars that were there already began, after years of mediocre trade, to flourish dramatically, while new ones opened one after the other.

The establishment that was to become the Migi-Hidari was known at that time simply as 'Yamagata's' – after its proprietor, an old veteran soldier – and was the longest-established bar in the district. It was a somewhat colourless place in those days, but I had used it regularly over the years since first coming to the city. As far as I recall, it was not until a few months after the arrival of the new tramlines that Yamagata saw what was happening around him, and began to formulate his ideas. With the area set to become a fully fledged drinking quarter, his own establishment – being the oldest, and situated as it was at the intersection of three streets – stood naturally to become a sort of patriarch among local establishments. In view of this, so he saw it, it was his responsibility to expand and re-open in grand style. The tradesman above him was ready to be bought out, and the necessary capital could be raised without difficulty. The main stumbling block, both as regards his own establishment and the district as a whole, was the attitude of the city authorities.

In this, Yamagata was undoubtedly correct. For this was 1933 or 1934 – an unlikely time, you may recall, to be contemplating the birth of a new pleasure district. The authorities had been applying arduous policies to keep the more frivolous side of the city's life in check, and indeed, in the city centre, many of the more decadent establishments were in the process of being closed down. At first, then, I did not listen to Yamagata's ideas with much sympathy. It was only when he told me just what sort of place he had in mind that I became sufficiently impressed and promised I would do what I could to help him.

I believe I have already mentioned the fact that I played a small part in the Migi-Hidari's coming into existence. Of course, not being a man of wealth, there was little I could do financially. But by that time my reputation in this city had grown to a certain extent; as I recall, I was not yet serving on the arts committee of the State Department, but I had many personal links there and was already being consulted frequently on matters of policy. So then, my petition to the authorities on Yamagata's behalf was not without weight.

'It is the owner's intention', I explained, 'that the proposed establishment be a celebration of the new patriotic spirit emerging in Japan today. The décor would reflect the new spirit, and any patron incompatible with that spirit would be firmly encouraged to leave. Furthermore, it is the owner's intention that the establishment be a place where this city's artists and writers whose works most reflect the new spirit can gather and drink together. With respect to this last point, I have myself secured the support of various of my colleagues, among them the painter, Masayuki Harada; the playwright, Misumi; the journalists, Shigeo Otsuji and Eiji Nastuki – all of them, as you will know, producers of work unflinchingly loyal to his Imperial Majesty the Emperor.'

I went on to point out how such an establishment, given its dominance in the neighbourhood, would be an ideal means by which to ensure that a desirable tone prevailed in the district.

'Otherwise,' I warned, 'I fear we are faced with the growth of another quarter characterized by the very sort of decadence we have been doing our best to combat and which we know so weakens the fibre of our culture.'

The authorities responded not simply with acquiescence, but with an enthusiasm that surprised me. It was, I suppose, another of those instances when one is struck by the realization that one is held in rather higher esteem than one supposed. But then I was never one to concern myself with matters of esteem, and this was not why the advent of the Migi-Hidari brought me so much personal satisfaction; rather, I was proud to see borne out something I had maintained for some time – namely that the new spirit of Japan was not incompatible with enjoying oneself; that is to say, there was no reason why pleasure-seeking had to go hand in hand with decadence.

So then, some two-and-a-half years after the coming of the new tramlines, the Migi-Hidari was opened. The renovations had been skilful and extensive, so that anyone strolling that way after dark could hardly fail to notice that brightly-lit front with its numerous lanterns, large and small, hung along the gables, under the eaves, in neat rows along the window ledges and above the main entryway; then, too, there was that enormous illuminated banner suspended from the ridge-pole bearing the new name of the premises against a background of army boots marching in formation.

One evening, shortly after its opening, Yamagata took me inside, told me to choose my favourite table, and declared that thereafter it was reserved for my sole use. Primarily, I suppose, this was in recognition of the small service I had done him. But then, of course, I had always been one of Yamagata's best customers.

Indeed, I had been going into Yamagata's for over twenty years prior to its transformation into the Migi-Hidari. This was not really through any deliberate choice on my part – as I say, it was an undistinguished sort of place – but when I first came to this city as a young man, I was living in Furukawa and Yamagata's place happened to be at hand.

It is perhaps hard for you to picture how ugly Furukawa was in those days. Indeed, if you are new to the city, my talking of the Furukawa district probably conjures up the park that stands there today and the peach trees for which it is renowned. But when I first came to this city – in 1913 – the area was full of factories and warehouses belonging to the smaller companies, many of them abandoned or in disrepair. The houses were old and shabby and the only people who lived in Furukawa were those who could afford only the lowest rents.

Mine was a small attic room above an old woman living with her unmarried son, and was quite unsuitable for my needs. There being no electricity in the house, I was obliged to paint by oil-light; there was barely enough space to set up an easel, and I could not avoid splashing the walls and tatami with paint; I would often wake the old woman or her son while working through the night; and most vexing of all, the attic ceiling was too low to allow me to stand up fully, so I would often work for hours in a half-crouched position, hitting my head continually on the rafters. But then in those days I was so delighted at having been accepted by the Takeda firm, and to be earning my living as an artist, that I gave little thought to these unhappy conditions.

During the day, of course, I did not work in my room, but at

Master Takeda's 'studio'. This, too, was in Furukawa, a long room above a restaurant – long enough, in fact, for all fifteen of us to set up easels all in a row. The ceiling, though higher than that in my attic room, sagged considerably at the centre, so that whenever we entered the room we always joked that it had descended a few more centimetres since the previous day. There were windows along the length of the room, and these should have given us a good light to work by; but somehow the shafts of sunlight that came in were always too sharp, giving the room something of the look of a ship's cabin. The other problem with the place was the fact that the restaurateur downstairs would not allow us to remain after six o'clock in the evening when his customers would begin to come in. 'You sound like a herd of cattle up there,' he would say. We would thus have no choice but to continue our work back at our respective lodgings.

I should perhaps explain that there was no chance of our completing our schedule without working in the evenings. The Takeda firm prided itself on its ability to provide a high number of paintings at very short notice; indeed, Master Takeda gave us to understand that if we failed to fulfil our deadline in time for the ship leaving harbour, we would quickly lose future commissions to rival firms. The result was that we would work the most arduous hours, late into the night, and still feel guilty the next day because we were behind schedule. Often, as the deadline date approached, it would not be unusual for us all to be living on just two or three hours of sleep each night, and painting around the clock. At times, if several commissions came in one after the next, we would be going from day to day dizzy with exhaustion. But for all that, I cannot recall our ever failing to complete a commission on time, and, I suppose, that gives some indication of the hold Master Takeda had over us.

After I had been with Master Takeda for a year or so, a new artist joined the firm. This was Yasunari Nakahara, a name which I doubt will mean much to you. In fact, there is no reason why you should have come across it, since he never achieved any kind of reputation. The most he did was eventually to gain a post as art teacher at a high school in the Yuyama district a few years before the war – a post, I am told, he still holds today, the authorities seeing no reason to replace him as they did so many of his fellow teachers. Myself, I always remember him as 'the Tortoise', the name given to him during those days at the Takeda firm, and one which I came to use affectionately throughout our friendship.

I have still in my possession a painting by the Tortoise – a self-portrait he painted not long after the Takeda days. It shows a thin young man with spectacles, sitting in his shirtsleeves in a cramped, shadowy room, surrounded by easels and rickety furniture, his face caught on one side by the light coming from the window. The earnestness and timidity written on the face are certainly true to the man I remember, and in this respect, the Tortoise has been remarkably honest; looking at the portrait, you would probably take him to be the sort you could confidently elbow aside for an empty tram seat. But then each of us, it seems, has his own special conceits. If the Tortoise's modesty forbade him to disguise his timid nature, it did not prevent him attributing to himself a kind of lofty intellectual air – which I for one have no recollection of. But then to be fair, I cannot recall any colleague who could paint a self-portrait with absolute honesty; however accurately one may fill in the surface details of one's mirror reflection, the personality represented rarely comes near the truth as others would see it.

The Tortoise earned his nickname because, joining the firm in the midst of a particularly busy commission, he proceeded to produce only two or three canvasses in the time it took the rest of us to complete six or seven. At first, his slowness was put down to inexperience and the nickname was used only behind his back. But as the weeks went by and his rate had not improved, the bitterness against him grew. It soon became commonplace for people to call him 'Tortoise' to his face, and although he fully realized the name was anything but affectionate, I remember him trying his best to take it as though it were. For instance, if someone called across the long room: 'Hey, Tortoise, are you still painting that petal you began last week?' he would make an effort to laugh as though to share in the joke. I recall my colleagues often attributing this apparent inability to defend his dignity to the fact that the Tortoise was from the Negishi district; for in those days, as today, there prevailed the rather unfair myth that those from that part of the city invariably grew up weak and spineless.

I remember one morning, when Master Takeda had left the long room for a moment, two of my colleagues going up to the Tortoise's easel and challenging him about his lack of speed. My easel stood not far from his, so I could see clearly the nervous expression on his face as he replied:

'I beg you to be patient with me. It is my greatest wish to learn from you, my superior colleagues, how to produce work of such quality so quickly. I have done my utmost in these past weeks to paint faster, but sadly I was forced to abandon several pictures, because the loss of quality on account of my hurrying was such that I would have disgraced the high standards of our firm. But I will do all I can to improve my poor standing in your eyes. I beg you to forgive me and to be patient a while longer.'

The Tortoise repeated this plea two or three times over, while his tormentors persisted with their abuse, accusing him of laziness and of relying on the rest of us to do his share of the work. By this time, most of us had ceased to paint and had gathered round. I believe it was after his accusers had begun to abuse the Tortoise in particularly harsh terms, and when I saw that the rest of my colleagues would do nothing but watch with a kind of fascination, that I stepped forward and said:

'That's enough, can't you see you're talking to someone with artistic integrity? If an artist refuses to sacrifice quality for the sake of speed, then that's something we should all respect. You've become fools if you can't see that.'

Of course, this is all a matter of many years ago now and I cannot vouch that those were my exact words that morning. But I spoke in some such way on the Tortoise's behalf, of that I am quite certain; for I can distinctly recall the gratitude and relief on the Tortoise's face as he turned to me, and the astonished stares of all the others present. I myself command-ed considerable respect amongst my colleagues – my own output being unchallengeable in terms either of quality or quantity – and I believe my intervention put an end to the Tortoise's ordeal at least for the rest of that morning.

You may perhaps think I am taking too much credit in relating this small episode; after all, the point I was making in the Tortoise's defence seems a very obvious one – one you may think would occur instantly to anyone with any respect for serious art. But it is necessary to remember the climate of those days at Master Takeda's – the feeling amongst us that we were all battling together against time to preserve the hard-earned reputation of the firm. We were also quite aware that the essential point about the sort of things we were commissioned to paint – geishas, cherry trees, swimming carps, temples – was that they look 'Japanese' to the foreigners to whom they were shipped out, and all finer points of style were quite likely to go unnoticed. So I do not think I am claiming undue credit for my younger self if I suggest my actions that day were a manifestation of a quality I came to be much respected for in later years – the ability to think and judge for myself, even if it meant going against the sway of those around me. The fact remains, certainly, that I was the only one to come to the Tortoise's defence that morning.

Although the Tortoise managed to thank me for that small intervention, and for subsequent acts of support, the pace of those days was such that it was some time before I was able to talk to him at length in any intimacy. Indeed, I believe almost two months had elapsed since the incident I have just related, when there came at last something of a lull in our frantic schedule. I was strolling around the grounds of Tamagawa temple, as I often did when I found some spare time, and spotted the Tortoise sitting on a bench in the sunshine, apparently asleep.

I remain an enthusiast of the Tamagawa grounds, and would agree that the hedges and rows of trees to be found there today may indeed help provide an atmosphere more in keeping with a place of worship. But whenever I go there now, I find myself becoming nostalgic for the Tamagawa grounds as they used to be. In those days, before the hedges and trees, the grounds seemed far more extensive and full of life; scattered all over the open expanse of green, you would see stalls selling candy and balloons, sideshows with jugglers or conjurers; the Tamagawa grounds were also the place to go, I remember, if you wanted a photograph made, for you could not stroll far without coming across a photographer camped in his stall with his tripod and dark cloak. The afternoon I found the Tortoise there was on a Sunday at the start of spring, and everywhere was busy with parents and children. He woke with a start as I walked over and sat next to him.

'Why, Ono-san!' he exclaimed, his face lighting up. 'What good fortune to see you today. Why, just a moment ago, I was saying to myself, if only I had a little spare money, I would buy something for Ono-san, some token of gratitude for his kindness to me. But for the moment I can only afford something cheap and that would be an insult. So in the meantime, Ono-san, let me just thank you from my heart for all you've done for me.'

'I've not done very much,' I said. 'I just spoke my mind a few times, that's all.'

'But truly, Ono-san, men like you are all too rare. It is an honour to be a colleague of such a man. However much our paths may part in years to come, I'll always remember your kindness.'

I recall having to listen for several more moments to his

praise of my courage and integrity. Then I said: 'I'd been meaning to talk to you for some time. You see, I've been thinking things over and I'm considering leaving Master Takeda in the near future.'

The Tortoise stared at me with astonishment. Then, comically, he looked about him as though in fear I had been overheard.

'I've been very fortunate,' I went on. 'My work has caught the interest of the painter and printmaker, Seiji Moriyama. You've heard of him, no doubt?'

The Tortoise, still staring at me, shook his head.

'Mr Moriyama,' I said, 'is a *true* artist. In all likelihood, a great one. I've been exceptionally fortunate to receive his attention and advice. Indeed, it's his opinion that my remaining with Master Takeda will do irreparable harm to my gifts, and he has invited me to become his pupil.'

'Is that so?' my companion remarked warily.

'And you know, as I was strolling through the park just now, I was thinking to myself: "Of course, Mr Moriyama is absolutely correct. It's all very well for the rest of those work-horses to toil under Master Takeda to earn their living. But those of us with serious ambitions must look elsewhere." '

At this point, I gave the Tortoise a meaningful glance. He continued to stare at me, a puzzled look entering his expression.

'I'm afraid I took the liberty of mentioning you to Mr Moriyama,' I told him. 'In fact, I expressed the opinion that you were the exception amongst my present colleagues. You alone among them had real talent and serious aspirations.'

'Really, Ono-san,' – he burst into laughter – 'how can you say such a thing? I know you mean to be kind to me, but this is going too far.'

'I've made up my mind to accept Mr Moriyama's kind offer,' I continued. 'And I urge you to let me show your work to him. With luck, you too may be invited to become his pupil.'

The Tortoise looked at me with distress on his face.

'But Ono-san, what are you saying?' he said in a lowered voice. 'Master Takeda took me on through the recommendation of a most respected acquaintance of my father. And really, he has shown me great tolerance, despite all my problems. How can I be so disloyal as to leave after only a few months?' Then suddenly, the Tortoise seemed to see the import of his words, and added hurriedly: 'But of course, Ono-san, I don't imply *you* are in any way disloyal. Circumstances are different in your case. I wouldn't presume . . .' He faded off into embarrassed giggling. Then with an effort, he pulled himself together to ask: 'Are you serious about leaving Master Takeda, Ono-san?'

'In my opinion,' I said, 'Master Takeda doesn't deserve the loyalty of the likes of you and me. Loyalty has to be earned. There's too much made of loyalty. All too often men talk of loyalty and follow blindly. I for one have no wish to lead my life like that.'

These, of course, may not have been the precise words I used that afternoon at the Tamagawa temple; for I have had cause to recount this particular scene many times before, and it is inevitable that with repeated telling, such accounts begin to take on a life of their own. But even if I did not express myself to the Tortoise quite so succinctly that day, I think it can be assumed those words I have just attributed to myself do represent accurately enough my attitude and resolve at that point in my life.

One place, incidentally, where I was obliged to tell and retell stories of those days at the Takeda firm was around that table in the Migi-Hidari; my pupils seemed to share a fascination for hearing about this early part of my career – perhaps because they were naturally interested to learn what their teacher was doing at their age. In any case, the topic of my days with Master Takeda would come up frequently during the course of those evenings.

'It wasn't such a bad experience,' I remember telling them

once. 'It taught me some important things.'

'Forgive me, Sensei,' – I believe it was Kuroda who leaned across the table to say this – 'but I find it hard to believe a place like the one you describe could teach an artist anything useful whatsoever.'

'Yes, Sensei,' said another voice, 'do tell us what a place like that could have possibly taught you. It sounds more like a firm producing cardboard boxes.'

This was the way things would go at the Migi-Hidari. I could be having a conversation with someone, the rest of them talking amongst themselves, and as soon as an interesting question had been asked of me, they would all break off their own conversations and I would have a circle of faces awaiting my reply. It was as though they never talked amongst themselves without having an ear open for another piece of knowledge I might impart. This is not to say that they were uncritical; quite the contrary, they were a brilliant set of young men and one would never dare say anything without first having thought about it.

'Being at Takeda's', I told them, 'taught me an important lesson early in my life. That while it was right to look up to teachers, it was always important to question their authority. The Takeda experience taught me never to follow the crowd blindly, but to consider carefully the direction in which I was being pushed. And if there's one thing I've tried to encourage you all to do, it's been to rise above the sway of things. To rise above the undesirable and decadent influences that have swamped us and have done so much to weaken the fibre of our nation these past ten, fifteen years.' No doubt I was a little drunk and sounded rather grandiose, but that was the way those sessions around that corner table went.

'Indeed, Sensei,' someone said, 'we must all remember that. We must all endeavour to rise above the sway of things.'

'And I think we here around this table,' I went on, 'have a right to be proud of ourselves. The grotesque and the frivolous have been prevalent all around us. But now at last a finer, more manly spirit is emerging in Japan and you here are part of it. In fact, it's my wish that you should go on to become recognized as nothing less than the spearhead of the new spirit. Indeed' – and by this point, I would be addressing not just those around the table, but all those listening nearby – 'this establishment of ours where we all gather is a testimony to the new emerging spirit and all of us here have a right to be proud.'

Frequently, as the drinking got merrier, outsiders would come crowding round our table to join in our arguments and speeches, or simply to listen and soak in the atmosphere. On the whole, my pupils were ready enough to give strangers a hearing, though of course, if we were imposed on by a bore, or by someone with disagreeable views, they would be quick to squeeze him out. But for all the shouting and speech-making that went on into the night, real quarrels were rare at the Migi-Hidari, all of us who frequented that place being united by the same essential spirit; that is to say, the establishment proved to be everything Yamagata had wished; it repre-sented something fine and one could get drunk there with pride and dignity.

I have somewhere in this house a painting by Kuroda, that most gifted of my pupils, depicting one such evening at the Migi-Hidari. It is entitled: 'The Patriotic Spirit', a title that may lead you to expect a work depicting soldiers on the march or some such thing. Of course, it was Kuroda's very point that a patriotic spirit began somewhere further back, in the routine of our daily lives, in such things as where we drank and who we mixed with. It was his tribute – for he believed in such things then – to the spirit of the Migi-Hidari. The picture, painted in oils, shows several tables and takes in much of the colour and décor of the place – most noticeably, the patriotic banners and slogans suspended from the rails of the upper balcony. Beneath the banners, guests are gathered around tables in conversation, while in the foreground a waitress in a kimono hurries with a tray of drinks. It is a fine painting, capturing very accurately the boisterous, yet somehow proud and respectable atmosphere of the Migi-Hidari. And whenever I happen to look at it today, it still brings me a certain satisfaction to recall that I – with whatever influence my reputation had gained in this city – was able to do my small part in bringing such a place into being.

Quite often these days, in the evenings down at Mrs Kawakami's, I find myself reminiscing about the Migi-Hidari and the old days. For there is something about Mrs Kawakami's place when Shintaro and I are the only customers there, something about sitting together up at the bar under those low-hung lights, that puts us in a nostalgic mood. We may start discussing someone from the past, about how much he could drink perhaps, or some funny mannerism he had. Then before long we will be trying to get Mrs Kawakami to recall the man, and in our attempts to jog her memory, we will find ourselves remembering more and more amusing things about him. The other night, after we had been laughing over just such a set of reminiscences, Mrs Kawakami said, as she often will do on these occasions: 'Well, I don't recall the name, but I'm sure I'd recognize his face.'

'Well in truth, Obasan,' I said, remembering, 'he was never a real customer here. He used to always drink across the street.'

'Oh yes, at the big place. Still, if I saw him, I may recognize him. But then again, who knows? People change so much. Every now and then, I see someone in the street, and I think I know them and I should greet them. But then I look at them again and I'm not so sure.'

'Why, Obasan,' Shintaro put in, 'just the other day, I greeted someone in the street, thinking it was someone I knew. But the man obviously thought I was a madman. He walked away without replying!'

Shintaro seemed to regard this as an amusing story and laughed loudly. Mrs Kawakami smiled, but did not join in his laughter. Then she turned to me and said:

'Sensei, you must try and persuade your friends to start coming back to these parts. In fact, perhaps each time we see an old face from those days, we should be stopping him and telling him to come here to this little place. That way we could start rebuilding the old days.'

'Now that's a splendid idea, Obasan,' I said. 'I'll try and remember to do that. I'll stop people in the street and say: "I remember you from the old days. You used to be a regular around our district. Well, you may think it's all gone, but you're wrong. Mrs Kawakami's is still there, the same as ever, and things are slowly building back up again." '

'That's it, Sensei,' Mrs Kawakami said. 'You tell them they'll be missing out. Business will start to improve then. After all, it's Sensei's duty to bring back the old crowd. Everyone always looked up to Sensei as the natural leader around here.'

'A good point, Obasan,' Shintaro said. 'In olden times, if a lord had his troops scattered after a battle, he'd soon go about gathering them together again. Sensei is in a similar position.'

'What nonsense,' I said, laughing.

'That's right, Sensei,' Mrs Kawakami went on, 'you find all the old people again and tell them to come back. Then after a while, I'll buy the place next door and we'll open up a grand old place. Just like that big place used to be.'

'Indeed, Sensei,' Shintaro was still saying. 'A lord must gather his men again.'

'An interesting idea, Obasan,' I said, nodding. 'And you know, the Migi-Hidari was just a small place once. No bigger than this place here. But then in time we managed to turn it into what it was. Well, perhaps we'll just have to do the same thing again with this place of yours. Now things are settling a little, the custom ought to be coming back.'

'You could bring in all your artist friends again, Sensei,' Mrs Kawakami said. 'Then before long, all the newspaper men will follow.'

'An interesting idea. We could probably pull it off. Except I wonder, Obasan. You may not be able to handle such a big place. We wouldn't want you getting out of your depth.'

'Nonsense,' Mrs Kawakami said, putting on an offended look. 'If Sensei will hurry up and do his part, you'll see how well things will be managed around here.'

Recently we have had such conversations over and over. And who is to say the old district will not return again? The likes of Mrs Kawakami and I, we may tend to make a joke about it, but behind our bantering there is a thread of serious optimism. 'A lord must gather his men.' And so perhaps he should. Perhaps, when Noriko's future is once and for all settled, I will give some serious consideration to Mrs Kawakami's schemes.

I suppose I might mention here that I have seen my former protégé, Kuroda, just once since the end of the war. It was quite by chance on a rainy morning during the first year of the occupation – before the Migi-Hidari and all those other buildings had been demolished. I was walking somewhere, making my way through what was left of our old pleasure district, looking from under my umbrella at those skeletal remains. I remember there were workmen wandering around that day, and so at first I paid no attention to the figure standing looking at one of the burnt-out buildings. It was only as I walked by that I became aware the figure had turned and was watching me. I paused, then looked around, and through the rain dripping off my umbrella, saw with a strange shock Kuroda looking expressionlessly towards me.

Beneath his umbrella, he was hatless and dressed in a dark raincoat. The charred buildings behind him were dripping and the remnant of some gutter was making a large amount of rainwater splash down not far from him. I remember a truck going by between us, full of building workers. And I noticed how one of the spokes of his umbrella was broken, causing some more splashing just beside his foot.

Kuroda's face, which had been quite round before the war, had hollowed out around the cheekbones, and what looked like heavy lines had appeared towards the chin and the throat. And I thought to myself as I stood there: 'He's not young any more.'

He moved his head very slightly. I was not sure if it was the beginning of a bow, or if he was just adjusting his head to get out of the splash of rainwater from his broken umbrella. Then he turned and began to walk off in the other direction.

But it was not my intention to dwell on Kuroda here. Indeed, he would not be on my mind at all had his name not turned up so unexpectedly last month, during the chance meeting on the tram with Dr Saito.

It was the afternoon I eventually took Ichiro to see his monster film – a trip he had been denied the previous day by Noriko's stubbornness. In fact, my grandson and I went by ourselves, Noriko refusing to come and Setsuko again volunteering to remain at home. It was, of course, simple childishness on Noriko's part, but Ichiro had his own interpretation of the women's behaviour. As we sat down to lunch that day, he continued to say:

'Aunt Noriko and Mother aren't coming. It's much too scaring for women. They'd be much too scared, isn't that right, Oji?'

'Yes, I expect that's right, Ichiro.'

'They'd be much too scared. Aunt Noriko, you'd be far too scared to see the film, wouldn't you?'

'Oh yes,' Noriko said, pulling a frightened face.

'Even Oji's scared. Look, you can see even Oji's scared. And he's a man.'

That afternoon, as I was standing at the end of the entry-way waiting to leave for the cinema, I witnessed a curious scene between Ichiro and his mother. While Setsuko was strapping up his sandals, I could see my grandson continually trying to say something to her. But whenever Setsuko said: 'What is it, Ichiro, I can't hear,' he would glare angrily, then cast a quick glance towards me to see if I had heard. Finally, once the sandals had been put on, Setsuko bent down so that Ichiro could whisper into her ear. She then nodded and disappeared into the house, returning a moment later with a raincoat, which she folded and handed to him.

'It's unlikely to rain,' I remarked, looking out beyond the front entrance. Indeed, it was a fine day outside.

'All the same,' Setsuko said, 'Ichiro would like to take it with him.'

I was puzzled by this insistence on the raincoat. Then once we were out in the sunshine, and making our way down the hill towards the tram stop, I noticed the swagger with which Ichiro walked – as though the coat slung through his arm had transformed him into someone like Humphrey Bogart – and concluded it was all in imitation of some comic-book hero of his.

I suppose we were almost at the bottom of the hill when Ichiro declared loudly: 'Oji, you used to be a famous artist.'

'I expect that's right, Ichiro.'

'I told Aunt Noriko to show me Oji's pictures. But she won't show me.'

'Hmm. They're all tidied away just for the moment.'

'Aunt Noriko's disobedient, isn't she, Oji? I told her to show me Oji's pictures. Why won't she show me?'

I laughed and said: 'I don't know, Ichiro. Perhaps she was busy with something.'

'She's disobedient.'

I gave another laugh, saying: 'I suppose so, Ichiro.'

The tram stop is ten minutes' walk from our house; down the hill to the river, then a little way along the new concrete embankment, and the northbound circuit joins the road just beyond the site of the new housing schemes. That sunny afternoon last month, my grandson and I boarded there for the city centre, and it was on that journey we encountered Dr Saito.

I realize I have said very little so far about the Saito family, the eldest son of which is presently involved in marriage talks with Noriko. The Saitos are, all in all, a very different sort of prospect from the Miyakes of last year. The Miyakes were, of course, decent enough people, but they could not, in all fairness, be called a family of any prestige, whereas the Saito family, without exaggeration, is just that. In fact, although Dr Saito and I were not properly acquainted before, I had always known of his activities in the world of the arts, and for years, whenever we had passed in the street, we had exchanged greetings politely to acknowledge our familiarity with each other's reputations. But of course, on the occasion on which we met last month, things had become very different.

The tram does not become crowded until it has crossed the river at the steel bridge opposite Tanibashi Station, and so, when Dr Saito boarded one stop after us, he was able to take a vacant seat beside me. Inevitably, our conversation began a little uncomfortably; for the negotiations were at an early, delicate stage, and it did not seem proper to discuss them openly; but then it would have been absurd to pretend they were not going on. In the end, we both praised the merits of 'our mutual friend, Mr Kyo' – the go-between in the proposal – and Dr Saito remarked with a smile: 'Let us hope his efforts bring us together again shortly.' And that was as close as we came to discussing the matter. I could not help noticing the marked contrast between the assured way Dr Saito had responded to the slightly awkward situation, and the nervous, clumsy way the Miyake family had handled things from start to finish last year. Whatever the eventual outcome, one does feel reassured to be dealing with the likes of the Saito family.

Otherwise, we talked mainly of small things. Dr Saito has a warm, genial manner, and when he leaned forward to ask Ichiro how he was enjoying his visit, and about the movie we were about to see, my grandson showed no inhibitions about conversing with him.

'A fine boy,' Dr Saito said to me, approvingly.

It was shortly before his stop – he had already put his hat back on – that Dr Saito remarked: 'We have another mutual acquaintance. A certain Mr Kuroda.'

I looked at him, a little startled. 'Mr Kuroda,' I repeated. 'Ah, no doubt that would be the same gentleman I once supervised.'

'That's right. I came across him recently and he happened to mention your name.'

'Is that so? I haven't come across him for some time. Not since before the war, certainly. How is Mr Kuroda these days? What is he up to?'

'I believe he is about to take up an appointment at the new Uemachi College, where he will teach art. This was how I came across him. I was kindly asked by the college to advise on the appointments board.'

'Ah, so you don't know Mr Kuroda well.'

'Indeed not. But I hope to see more of him in future.'

'Is that so?' I said. 'So Mr Kuroda still remembers me. How good of him.'

'Yes, indeed. He mentioned your name when we happened to be discussing something. I've not had the opportunity to talk to him at any length. But should I see him again, I'll mention that I saw you.'

'Ah, indeed.'

The tram was crossing the steel bridge and the wheels made a loud clanging noise. Ichiro, who had been kneeling on his seat to see out of the window, pointed out something down in the water. Dr Saito turned to look, exchanged a few more words with Ichiro, then got to his feet as his stop approached. He made a last allusion to 'the efforts of Mr Kyo' before bowing and making his way to the exit.

As usual, many people crowded on at the stop after the bridge, and the rest of our journey was rather uncomfortable. When we got off just in front of the cinema, I could see the poster prominently displayed at the entrance. My grandson had achieved a close likeness in his sketch of two days earlier, though there was no fire in the picture; what Ichiro had remembered were the impact lines – resembling streaks of lightning – which the artist had painted in to emphasize the ferocity of the giant lizard.

Ichiro went up to the poster and burst into loud laughter.

'It's easy to see that's a made-up monster,' he said, pointing. 'Anyone can see that. It's just made up.' And he laughed again.

'Ichiro, please don't laugh so loudly. Everyone's looking at you.'

'But I can't help it. The monster looks so made up. Who'd be scared of a thing like that?'

It was only once we were seated inside, and the film had begun, that I discovered the true purpose of his raincoat. Ten minutes into the film, we heard ominous music and on the screen appeared a dark cave with mist swirling about it. Ichiro whispered: 'This is boring. Will you tell me when something interesting starts to happen?' And with that, he threw the raincoat over his head. A moment later, there was a roar and the giant lizard emerged from the cave. Ichiro's hand was clutching at my arm, and when I glanced at him his other hand was holding the raincoat in place as tightly as possible.

The coat continued to cover his head for more or less the whole duration of the film. Occasionally, my arm would be shaken and a voice would ask from underneath: 'Is it getting interesting yet?' I would then be obliged to describe in whispers what was on the screen until a small gap appeared in the raincoat. But within minutes – at the slightest hint that the monster would reappear – the gap would close and his voice would say: 'This is boring. Don't forget to tell me when it gets interesting.'

When we got home, though, Ichiro was full of enthusiasm for the film. 'The best movie I've ever seen,' he continued to say, and he was still giving us his version of it when we sat down to supper.

'Aunt Noriko, shall I tell you what happened next? It gets very scary. Shall I tell you?'

'I'm getting so frightened, Ichiro, I can hardly eat,' Noriko said.

'I'm warning you, it gets even more frightening. Shall I tell you more?'

'Oh, I'm not sure, Ichiro. You've got me so frightened already.'

It had not been my intention to make heavy talk at the supper table by bringing up Dr Saito, but then it would have been unnatural not to mention our meeting when recounting the day's events. So, when Ichiro paused a moment, I said: 'Incidentally, we met Dr Saito on the tram. He was travelling up to see someone.'

When I said this, my two daughters both stopped eating and looked at me with surprise.

'But we didn't talk about anything significant,' I said, with a small laugh. 'Really. We just exchanged pleasantries, that's all.'

My daughters seemed unconvinced, but they began to eat again. Noriko glanced over to her elder sister, then Setsuko said: 'Dr Saito was well?'

'He appeared to be.'

We ate on quietly for a while. Perhaps Ichiro began to talk about the movie again. In any case, it was a little later in the meal that I said:

'An odd thing. It turns out Dr Saito met a former pupil of mine. Kuroda, in fact. It seems Kuroda's taking up a post at the new college.'

I looked up from my bowl and saw my daughters had again stopped eating. It was clear they had just exchanged glances, and it was one of those instances last month when I got a distinct impression they had at some point been discussing certain things about me.

That night, my two daughters and I were sitting around the table again, reading our newspapers and magazines, when we were disturbed by a dull thudding noise coming rhythmically from somewhere within the house. Noriko looked up in alarm, but Setsuko said:

'It's just Ichiro. He does that when he can't fall asleep.'

'Poor Ichiro,' Noriko said. 'I expect he keeps dreaming of the monster. It was so wicked of Father to take him to see a film like that.'

'Nonsense,' I said. 'He enjoyed it.'

'I think Father just wanted to see it himself,' Noriko said to her sister with a grin. 'Poor Ichiro. Being dragged along to a nasty film like that.'

Setsuko turned towards me with an embarrassed look. 'It was so kind of Father to take Ichiro,' she murmured.

'But now he can't sleep,' Noriko said. 'Ridiculous to take him to a film like that. No, you stay, Setsuko. I'll go.'

Setsuko watched her sister leave the room, then said:

'Noriko is so good with children. Ichiro will miss her when we go home.'

'Yes, indeed.'

'She was always good with children. Do you remember, Father, how she used to play those games with the Kinoshitas' little children?'

'Yes, indeed,' I said, with a laugh. Then I added: 'The Kinoshita boys are far too big these days to want to come around here.'

'She's always been so good with children,' Setsuko repeated. 'How sad to see her reach this age and still unmarried.'

'Indeed. The war came at a bad time for her.'

For a few moments we continued with our reading. Then Setsuko said:

'It was fortuitous to have met Dr Saito on the tram this afternoon. He sounds an admirable gentleman.'

'He is indeed. And from all accounts, the son is well worthy of his father.'

'Is that so?' Setsuko said, thoughtfully.

We returned to our reading for a few more moments. Then my daughter again broke the silence.

'And Dr Saito is acquainted with Mr Kuroda?'

'Only slightly,' I said, not looking up from my paper. 'It seems they met somewhere.'

'I wonder how Mr Kuroda is these days. I can remember how he used to come here, and you would talk together for hours in the reception room.'

'I've no idea about Kuroda these days.'

'Forgive me, but I wonder if it may not be wise if Father were to visit Mr Kuroda soon.'

'Visit him?'

'Mr Kuroda. And perhaps certain other such acquaintances from the past.'

'I'm not sure I follow what you're saying, Setsuko.'

'Forgive me, I simply meant to suggest that Father may wish to speak to certain acquaintances from his past. That is to say, before the Saitos' detective does. After all, we do not wish any unnecessary misunderstandings to arise.'

'No, I suppose we don't,' I said, returning to my paper.

I believe we did not discuss the matter further after that. Neither did Setsuko raise it again for the remainder of her stay last month.

Yesterday, as I took the tram down to Arakawa, the carriage was filled with bright autumn sunshine. I had not made the journey to Arakawa for a little while – in fact, not since the end of the war – and as I gazed out of my window, I noticed many changes in what had once been familiar scenery. Passing through Tozaka-cho and Sakaemachi, I could see brick apartment blocks looming above the small wooden houses I remembered from before. Then, as we passed the backs of the factories in Minamimachi, I saw how abandoned many of them had become; one factory yard went by after another, untidily stacked with broken timber, old sheets of corrugated metal, and often what looked to be plain rubble.

But then, after the tramline crosses the river at the THK Corporation Bridge, the atmosphere changes dramatically. You are travelling amidst fields and trees, and before long, the suburb of Arakawa will become visible at the bottom of the long steep hill where the tramline ends. The tram will move very slowly down the hill, then brake to a halt, and as you step out on to those cleanly swept pavements, you will be overcome by the distinct feeling you have left the city behind.

Arakawa, I have heard, completely escaped the bombings; and indeed, yesterday the place looked just as it had always done. A short walk up a hill, pleasantly shaded by cherry trees, brought me to Chishu Matsuda's house and that too was quite unchanged.

Matsuda's house, not as large or full of eccentricity as my own, is typical of the sort of solid, respectable house to be found in Arakawa. It stands on its own grounds, circled by a board fence, at a reasonable distance from the neighbouring properties: at the gateway, there is a bush of azaleas and a thick post sunk in the ground giving the family inscriptions. I pulled the bell and was answered by a woman of around forty whom I did not recognize. She showed me into the reception room, where she slid back the screen to the veranda, allowing the sun to enter and giving me a glimpse of the garden outside. Then she left me, saying: 'Mr Matsuda will not be a moment.'

I had first met Matsuda while living at Seiji Moriyama's villa, where the Tortoise and I had gone after leaving the Takeda firm. In fact, when Matsuda first came to the villa that day, I must already have been living there for some six years. It had been raining throughout the morning, and a group of us had been passing the time drinking and playing cards in one of the rooms. Then shortly after lunch, just as we had opened another large bottle, we heard a stranger's voice calling out in the yard.

The voice was strong and assured, and we all of us fell

silent and looked at each other in panic. For the fact was we had all leapt to the same thought – that the police had come to reprimand us. This was of course an utterly irrational idea, for we had not committed any sort of crime. And had, say, someone challenged our lifestyle during a conversation in a bar, any one of us would have been able to put up a spirited defence on its behalf. But that firm voice calling 'Anyone home?' had caught us unawares, causing us to betray our sense of guilt concerning our late nights of drinking, the way we slept through many of our mornings, the way we lived a life without routine in a decaying villa.

It was some moments then before one of my companions nearest the screen opened it, exchanged a few words with the caller, then turned and said: 'Ono, a gentleman wishes to speak with you.'

I went out on to the veranda to find a lean-featured young man of around my own age standing in the middle of the large square yard. I have retained a vivid picture of that first time I saw Matsuda. The rain had stopped and the sun was out. All around him were puddles of water and wet leaves fallen from the cedar trees overlooking the villa. He was dressed too dandyishly to be a policeman; his overcoat was sharply tailored with a high upturned collar, and he wore his hat slanted down over his eyes in a somewhat mocking manner. As I emerged, he was glancing around with interest at his surroundings, and something in the way he did this immediately suggested to me, that first time I saw him, Matsuda's arrogant nature. He saw me and came unhurriedly towards the veranda.

'Mr Ono?'

I asked what I could do for him. He turned, cast his eyes around the grounds again, then smiled up at me.

'An interesting place. This must have been a grand building once. Owned by a lord of some sort.'

'Indeed.'

'Mr Ono, my name is Chishu Matsuda. We have, in fact,

been in correspondence. I work for the Okada-Shingen Society.'

The Okada-Shingen Society no longer exists today – one of many such victims of the occupying forces – but quite possibly you will have heard of it, or at least of the exhibition it held each year until the war. The Okada-Shingen exhibition was for a time the principal means in this city by which artists emerging in painting and printmaking came to win public acclaim. Indeed, such was its reputation that in its latter years, most of the city's leading artists were displaying their latest works there alongside those of the newer talents. It was in connection with this same exhibition that the Okada-Shingen Society had written to me a few weeks prior to the afternoon of Matsuda's visit.

'I was made a little curious by your reply, Mr Ono,' Matsuda said. 'So I thought I'd call by and discover what it was all about.'

I looked at him coldly and said: 'I believe I made all the necessary points in my letter of reply. It was, however, most kind of you to have approached me.'

A slight smile appeared around his eyes. 'Mr Ono,' he said, 'it seems to me you are forgoing an important opportunity to enhance your reputation. So please tell me, when you insist you wish to have nothing to do with us, is that your own personal opinion? Or is it what your teacher happened to decree?'

'Naturally, I sought my teacher's advice. I am perfectly confident that the decision conveyed in my recent letter is the correct one. It was very good of you to come out here, but unfortunately I am occupied at this moment and cannot ask you to step up. I'll therefore bid you a good day.'

'One moment please, Mr Ono,' Matsuda said, his smile looking ever more mocking. He took a few more steps, coming right up to the veranda, and looked up at me. 'To be frank, I am not bothered about the exhibition. There are many others worthy of it. I came here, Mr Ono, because I wished to meet you.'

'Really? How good of you.'

'Indeed. I wished to say I am very struck by what I have seen of your work. I believe you have much talent.'

'You're most kind. No doubt I owe much to the excellence of my teacher's guidance.'

'No doubt. Now, Mr Ono, let us forget this exhibition. You must appreciate I do not merely work for the Okada-Shingen as a kind of clerk. I am a true lover of art. I have my beliefs and passions. And when every once in a while I come across a talent that truly excites me, then I feel I must do something about it. I would very much like to discuss certain ideas with you, Mr Ono. Ideas which may never have occurred to you before, but which I modestly suggest will be of benefit to your development as an artist. But I'll keep you no longer for the moment. Let me at least leave my calling card.'

He took his card from his wallet, placed it on the edge of the veranda, then with a quick bow, took his leave. But before he was half-way across the yard, he turned and called to me: 'Please consider my request carefully, Mr Ono. I merely wish to discuss certain ideas with you, that's all.'

That was almost thirty years ago, when we were both young and ambitious. Yesterday, Matsuda looked a very different man. His body has become broken down by ill-health, and his once handsome, arrogant face has become distorted by a lower jaw that seems no longer able to align itself with the upper. The woman who had answered the door to me helped him into the room and assisted him to sit down. When we were alone, Matsuda looked at me and said:

'You seem to have preserved your health well. As for myself, you can see I've deteriorated even further since our last meeting.'

I expressed sympathy, but stated he did not look as bad as all that.

'Don't try and fool me, Ono,' he said with a smile. 'I know

exactly how feeble I'm growing. There's little to be done, apparently. I have to just wait and see if my body recovers or else goes on getting worse. Still, enough about such cheerless matters. This is something of a surprise, to have you visit me again. I suppose we didn't part on the easiest of terms.'

'Really? But I wasn't aware we'd quarrelled.'

'Of course not. Why would we quarrel? I'm glad you've come to see me again. It must be three years since we last saw each other.'

'I believe so. It wasn't my intention to avoid you. I'd been meaning for some time to come out and pay a visit. But what with one thing and another . . .'

'Naturally,' he said. 'You had a lot to attend to. You must forgive me, of course, for failing to attend Michiko-san's funeral. I'd meant to write and express my apologies. The fact of the matter is, I didn't hear what had occurred until several days later. And then, of course, my own health . . .'

'Naturally, naturally. Indeed, I'm sure she would have been embarrassed by a large ostentatious ceremony. In any case, she would have known your thoughts would have been with her.'

'I can remember when you and Michiko-san were brought together.' He gave a laugh, nodding to himself. 'I was very happy for you that day, Ono.'

'Indeed,' I said, also laughing. 'You were to all intents our go-between. That uncle of yours just couldn't cope with the job.'

'That's right,' Matsuda said, smiling, 'you're bringing it all back to me. He'd get so embarrassed, he couldn't say or do anything without flushing scarlet. You remember that marriage meeting at the Yanagimachi Hotel?'

We both laughed. Then I said:

'You did a lot on our behalf. I doubt if it would have been brought off without you. Michiko always thought of you with gratitude.'

'A cruel thing,' Matsuda said, sighing. 'And with the war

all but over. I heard it was something of a freak raid.'

'Indeed. Hardly anyone else was hurt. It was as you say, a cruel thing.'

'But I'm bringing back terrible thoughts, I'm sorry.'

'Not at all. It's something of a comfort to remember her with you. I remember her back in the old days then.'

'Indeed.'

The woman brought in the tea. As she was laying down the tray, Matsuda said to her: 'Miss Suzuki, this is an old colleague of mine. We were very close once.'

She turned to me and bowed.

'Miss Suzuki doubles as my housekeeper and nurse,' Matsuda said. 'She's responsible for the fact that I'm still breathing.'

Miss Suzuki gave a laugh, bowed again and took her leave.

For a few moments after she had gone, Matsuda and I sat quietly, both gazing out between the screens Miss Suzuki had opened earlier. From where I sat, a pair of straw sandals were visible, left out on the veranda in the sun. But I could not see much of the garden itself, and for a moment felt tempted to rise to my feet and go out on the veranda. But realizing Matsuda would wish to accompany me and find difficulty doing so, I remained seated, wondering to myself if the garden was as it had been. As I remembered it, Matsuda's garden, though small, was arranged with much taste: a floor of smooth moss, a few small shapely trees and a deep pond. While sitting with Matsuda, I had caught an occasional splashing sound coming from outside and I was about to ask him if he still kept carp, when he said:

'I wasn't exaggerating when I told you Miss Suzuki was responsible for my life. She's been quite crucial on more than one occasion. You see, Ono, despite everything, I managed to hold on to some savings and assets. As a result, I'm able to employ her. Not so lucky for some others. I'm not exactly wealthy, but then, if I knew an old colleague was in difficulties, I'd do what I could to assist. After all, I have no children to leave money to.'

I gave a laugh. 'Same old Matsuda. Very forthright. It's kind of you, but that's not what brought me here. I too managed to hold on to my assets.'

'Ah, I'm pleased to hear that. You remember Nakane, the principal at Minami Imperial College? I see him from time to time. These days he's little better than a beggar. Of course, he tries to keep up appearances, but he lives entirely off borrowed money.'

'How terrible.'

'Some very unjust things have occurred,' Matsuda said. 'Still, we both managed to hold on to our assets. And you have more reason to be thankful, Ono. You appear to have held on to your health.'

'Indeed,' I said. 'I have much to be thankful for.'

Again, a splashing sound came from the pond outside, and it occurred to me it could be birds bathing at the water's edge.

'Your garden sounds distinctly different to mine,' I remarked. 'I can tell just listening to it that we're out of the city.'

'Is that so? I hardly remember what the city sounds like. This has been the extent of my world for the past few years. This house and this garden.'

'As a matter of fact, I did come to ask your help. But not in the way you implied earlier.'

'I see you've taken offence,' he said, nodding. 'Much the same as ever.'

We both laughed. Then he said: 'So what can I do for you?'

'The fact is,' I said, 'Noriko, my younger daughter, is at this moment involved in marriage talks.'

'Is that so?'

'To be frank, I'm a little concerned for her. She's already twenty-six. The war made things difficult for her. Otherwise, there's no doubting she'd have been married by now.'

'I believe I recall Miss Noriko. But she was just a little girl.

Twenty-six already. As you say, the war has made things difficult, even for the best prospects.'

'She was almost married last year,' I said, 'but the talks fell through at the last moment. I wonder, while we're on the subject, did anyone approach you last year concerning Noriko? I don't mean to be impertinent, but . . .'

'Not impertinent in the least, I quite understand. But no, I never spoke to anyone. But then I was very ill this time last year. If some detective had appeared, Miss Suzuki would no doubt have sent him away.'

I nodded, then said: 'It's just possible someone may call on you this year.'

'Oh? Well, I'll only have the best things to say about you. After all, we were good colleagues once.'

'I'm very grateful.'

'It's good of you to have called like this,' he said. 'But so far as Miss Noriko's marriage is concerned, it was quite unnecessary. We may not have parted on the easiest of terms, but things like that shouldn't come between us. Naturally, I'd say only the best things about you.'

'I didn't doubt it,' I said. 'You were always a generous man.'

'Still, if it's brought us together again, I'm glad.'

With some effort, Matsuda reached forward and began to refill our teacups. 'Forgive me, Ono,' he said, eventually, 'but you still seem uneasy about something.'

'I do?'

'Forgive me for putting it so bluntly, but the fact is very soon Miss Suzuki will be coming in to warn me I should retire again. I'm afraid I'm not able to entertain guests for prolonged periods, not even old colleagues.'

'Of course, I'm very sorry. It's most inconsiderate of me.'

'Don't be ridiculous, Ono. You can't go for a while yet. I was saying this because if you came here with a particular point to raise, it would be best if you'd do so soon.' Suddenly, he burst into laughter, saying: 'Really, you look aghast at my bad manners.'

'Not at all. It's most inconsiderate of me. But the truth is, I came simply to talk about my daughter's marriage prospects.'

'I see.'

'But I suppose,' I continued, 'it was my intention to mention certain eventualities. You see, the present negotiations may be quite delicate in nature. I'd be extremely beholden to you if you'd answer any queries which may come your way with delicacy.'

'Of course.' His gaze was on me, and there was a touch of amusement in his eyes. 'With utmost delicacy.'

'Particularly, that is, with regards to the past.'

'But I've said already,' Matsuda said, and his voice had become a little colder, 'I have only the best of things to report of you from the past.'

'Of course.'

Matsuda continued to look at me for a while, then he sighed.

'I've hardly moved from this house for the last three years,' he said. 'But I still keep my ears open for what's happening in this country of ours. I realize there are now those who would condemn the likes of you and me for the very things we were once proud to have achieved. And I suppose this is why you're worried, Ono. You think perhaps I will praise you for things perhaps best forgotten.'

'No such thing,' I said hastily. 'You and I both have a lot to be proud of. It's merely that where marriage talks are concerned, one has to appreciate the delicacy of the situation. But you've put my mind at rest. I know you'll exercise your judgement as well as ever.'

'I will do my best,' Matsuda said. 'But, Ono, there are things we should both be proud of. Never mind what people today are all saying. Before long, a few more years, and the likes of us will be able to hold our heads high about what we tried to do. I simply hope I live as long as that. It's my wish to see my life's efforts vindicated.'

'Of course. I feel quite same. But in respect to marriage

negotiations . . .'

'Naturally', Matsuda broke in, 'I'll do my best to exercise delicacy.'

I bowed, and we fell silent for a moment. Then he said:

'But tell me, Ono, if it's the case that you're worried about the past, I assume you've been visiting a few of the others from those days?'

'In fact, you're the first I've come to. I've no idea where many of our old friends are these days.'

'What about Kuroda? I hear he's living in the city somewhere.'

'Is that so? I haven't been in touch with him since . . . since the war.'

'If we're worrying about Miss Noriko's future, perhaps you'd best seek him out, painful as it may be.'

'Indeed. It's simply that I have no idea where he is.'

'I see. Hopefully their detective will be equally lost as to where to find him. But then sometimes those detectives can be very resourceful.'

'Indeed.'

'Ono, you look deathly pale. And you looked so healthy when you first arrived. That's what comes of sharing a room with a sickly man.'

I laughed and said: 'Not at all. It's just that one's children can be a great worry.'

Matsuda sighed again and said: 'People sometimes tell me I've missed out on life because I never married and had children. But when I look around me, children seem to be nothing but worry.'

'That's not far from the truth.'

'Still,' he said, 'it would be a comfort to think one had children to leave one's assets to.'

'Indeed.'

A few minutes later, as Matsuda had predicted, Miss Suzuki came in and said something to him. Matsuda smiled and said with resignation:

'My nurse has come to fetch me. Of course, you're welcome to remain here as long as you wish. But you must excuse me, Ono.'

Later, as I waited at the terminus for a tram to take me up the steep hill and back into the city, I felt a certain comfort in recalling Matsuda's assurance that he would have 'only the best of things to report from the past'. Of course, I could have been reasonably confident of this without my having gone to visit him. But then again, it is always good to re-establish contact with old colleagues. All in all, yesterday's trip to Arakawa was surely well worthwhile.

APRIL, 1949

On three or four evenings a week I still find myself taking that path down to the river and the little wooden bridge still known to some who lived here before the war as 'the Bridge of Hesitation'. We called it that because until not so long ago, crossing it would have taken you into our pleasure district, and conscience-troubled men – so it was said – were to be seen hovering there, caught between seeking an evening's entertainment and returning home to their wives. But if sometimes I am to be seen up on that bridge, leaning thoughtfully against the rail, it is not that I am hesitating. It is simply that I enjoy standing there as the sun sets, surveying my surroundings and the changes taking place around me.

Clusters of new houses have appeared towards the foot of the hill down which I have just come. And further along the riverbank, where a year ago there was only grass and mud, a city corporation is building apartment blocks for future employees. But these are still far from completion, and when the sun is low over the river, one might even mistake them for the bombed ruins still to be found in certain parts of this city.

But then such ruins become more and more scarce each week; indeed, one would probably have to go as far north as the Wakamiya district, or else to that badly struck area between Honcho and Kasugamachi to encounter them now in any number. But only a year ago, I am sure bombed ruins were still a commonplace sight all over this city. For instance, that area across from the Bridge of Hesitation – that area where our pleasure district had been – was this time last year still a desert of rubble. But now, work progresses there steadily every day. Outside Mrs Kawakami's, where once throngs of pleasure-seekers had squeezed past one another, a wide concrete road is being built, and along both sides of it, the foundations for rows of large office buildings.

I suppose by the time Mrs Kawakami informed me one evening not so long ago of the corporation's offer to buy her out for a generous sum, I had long since accepted she would sooner or later have to close up and move.

'I don't know what I should do,' she had said to me. 'It would be terrible to leave here after all this time. I was awake thinking about it all last night. But then again, Sensei, when I thought about it, I said to myself, well, now with Shintaro-san gone, Sensei's the only dependable customer I have left. I really don't know what I should do.'

I am indeed her only real customer these days; Shintaro has not shown his face at Mrs Kawakami's since that small episode last winter – lacking the courage, no doubt, to face me. This was, I suppose, unfortunate for Mrs Kawakami, who had had nothing to do with the affair.

It had been one evening last winter, while we were drinking together as was usual then, that Shintaro first mentioned to me his ambition to gain a teaching post at one of the new high schools. He then went on to reveal that in fact he had already made several applications for such posts. Now it is, of course, many years since Shintaro was my pupil, and there is no reason why he should not have gone about such matters without consulting me; I was fully aware there were others now – his employer, for instance – far more suitably placed to act as guarantor in such matters. Nevertheless, I confess I was somewhat surprised he should not have confided in me at all about these applications. And so, when Shintaro presented himself at my house that winter's day shortly after New Year, when I found him standing giggling nervously in my entry-way, saying: 'Sensei, it is a great impertinence of me to come here like this,' I felt something akin to relief, as though things were returning to a more familiar footing.

In the reception room I lit a brazier, and we both sat over it warming our hands. I noticed some snowflakes melting on the overcoat Shintaro was continuing to wear, and asked him:

'The snow has started again?'

'Just a little, Sensei. Nothing like this morning.'

'I'm sorry it's so cold in here. The coldest room in the house, I fear.'

'Not at all, Sensei. My own rooms are far colder.' He smiled happily and rubbed his hands together over the charcoal. 'It's good of you to receive me like this. Sensei has been very good to me over the years. I cannot begin to calculate what you have done for me.'

'Not at all, Shintaro. In fact, I sometimes think I rather neglected you in the old days. So if there's some way I can redeem my negligence, even at this late stage, I'd be pleased to hear of it.'

Shintaro laughed and went on rubbing his hands. 'Really, Sensei, you say the most absurd things. I can never begin to calculate what you have done for me.'

I watched him for a moment, then said: 'So tell me, Shintaro, what is it I can do for you?'

He looked up with a surprised expression, then laughed again.

'Excuse me, Sensei. I was getting so comfortable here, I'd quite forgotten my purpose in coming to trouble you like this.'

He was, he told me, most optimistic about his application to Higashimachi High School; reliable sources gave him to believe it was being viewed with much favour.

'However, Sensei, there appear to be just one or two small points on which the committee seem still a little unsatisfied.'

'Oh?'

'Indeed, Sensei. Perhaps I should be frank. The small points I refer to concern the past.'

'The past?'

'Indeed, Sensei.' At this point, Shintaro gave a nervous laugh. Then with an effort, he continued: 'You must know,

Sensei, that my respect for you is of the very highest. I have learnt so much from Sensei, and I will continue to be proud of our association.'

I nodded and waited for him to go on.

'The fact is, Sensei, I would be most grateful if you would yourself write to the committee, just to confirm certain statements I have made.'

'And what sort of statements are these, Shintaro?'

Shintaro gave another giggle, then reached his hands out over the brazier again.

'It is simply to satisfy the committee, Sensei. Nothing more. You may recall, Sensei, how we once had cause to disagree. Over the matter of my work during the China crisis.'

'The China crisis? I'm afraid I don't recall our quarrelling, Shintaro.'

'Forgive me, Sensei, perhaps I exaggerate. It was never as pronounced a thing as a quarrel. But I did indeed have the indiscretion to express my disagreement. That is to say, I resisted your suggestions concerning my work.'

'Forgive me, Shintaro, I don't recall what it is you're referring to.'

'No doubt such a trivial matter would not remain in Sensei's mind. But as it happens, it is of some importance to me at this juncture. You may remember better if I remind you of the party we had that night, the party to celebrate Mr Ogawa's engagement. It was that same night – I believe we were at the Hamabara Hotel – I perhaps drank a little too much and had the rudeness to express my views to you.'

'I have a vague recollection of that night, but I cannot say I remember it clearly. Still, Shintaro, what has a small disagreement like that to do with anything now?'

'Forgive me, Sensei, but as it happens, the matter has come to have some significance. The committee is obliged to be reassured of certain things. After all, there are the American authorities to satisfy . . .' Shintaro trailed off nervously. Then he said: 'I beg you, Sensei, to try and recall that little disagreement. Grateful as I was – and still remain – for the wealth of things I learnt under your supervision, I did not always, in fact, concur with your view. Indeed, I may not be exaggerating to say that I had strong reservations about the direction our school was taking at that time. You may recall, for instance, that despite my eventually following your instructions over the China crisis posters, I had misgivings and indeed went so far as to make my views known to you.'

'The China crisis posters,' I said, thinking to myself. 'Yes, I remember your posters now. It was a crucial time for the nation. A time to stop dithering and decide what we wanted. As I recall, you did well and we were all proud of your work.'

'But you will recall, Sensei, I had serious misgivings about the work you wished me to do. If you will recall, I openly expressed my disagreement that evening at the Hamabara Hotel. Forgive me, Sensei, for worrying you with such a trivial matter.'

I suppose I remained silent for some moments. I must have stood up at around this point, for when I next spoke, I recall I was standing across the room from him, over by the veranda screens.

'You wish me to write a letter to your committee,' I said eventually, 'disassociating you from my influence. This is what your request amounts to.'

'Nothing of the sort, Sensei. You misunderstand. I am as proud as ever to be associated with your name. It's simply that over the matter of the China poster campaign, if the committee could just be reassured . . .'

He trailed off again. I slid open a screen just far enough to form a tiny gap. Cold air came blowing into the room, but for some reason this did not concern me. I gazed through the gap, across the veranda and out into the garden. The snow was falling in slow drifting flakes.

'Shintaro,' I said, 'why don't you simply face up to the past? You gained much credit at the time for your poster campaign. Much credit and much praise. The world may now have a different opinion of your work, but there's no need to lie about yourself.'

'Indeed, Sensei,' Shintaro said. 'I take your point. But getting back to the matter in hand, I would be most grateful if you would write to the committee concerning the China crisis posters. In fact, I have here with me the name and address of the committee chairman.'

'Shintaro, please listen to me.'

'Sensei, with every respect, I am always very grateful for your advice and learning. But at this moment, I am a man in the midst of my career. It is all very well to reflect and ponder when one is in retirement. But as it happens, I live in a busy world and there are one or two things I must see to if I am to secure this post, which by all other counts is mine already. Sensei, I beg you, please consider my position.'

I did not reply, but continued to look out at the snow falling on my garden. Behind me, I could hear Shintaro getting to his feet.

'Here is the name and address, Sensei. If I may, I will leave them here. I would be most grateful if you would give the matter due consideration when you have a little time.'

There was a pause while, I suppose, he waited to see if I would turn and allow him to take his leave with some dignity. I went on gazing at my garden. For all its steady fall, the snow had settled only very lightly on the shrubs and branches. Indeed, as I watched, a breeze shook a branch of the maple tree, shaking off most of the snow. Only the stone lantern at the back of the garden had a substantial cap of white on it.

I heard Shintaro excuse himself and leave the room.

It may perhaps appear as if I was unnecessarily hard on Shintaro that day. But then if one bears in mind what had been taking place in the weeks immediately prior to that visit of his, it is surely understandable why I should have felt so unsympathetic towards his efforts to shirk his responsibilities.

For in fact, Shintaro's visit had come only a few days after Noriko's *miai*.

The negotiations around Noriko's proposed marriage to Taro Saito had progressed successfully enough throughout last autumn; an exchange of photographs had taken place in October and we had subsequently received word via Mr Kyo, our go-between, that the young man was keen to meet Noriko. Noriko, of course, made a show of thinking this over, but by that point, it had become obvious that my daughter – already twenty-six – could hardly pass over lightly a prospect like Taro Saito.

I thus informed Mr Kyo that we were agreeable to a *miai*, and eventually a date in November and the Kasuga Park Hotel were agreed upon. The Kasuga Park Hotel, you may agree, has these days a certain vulgar air about it, and I was somewhat unhappy with the choice. But then Mr Kyo had assured me a private room would be booked, and had gone on to suggest that the Saitos were much fond of the food there, and I finally gave my consent, albeit without enthusiasm.

Mr Kyo had also made the point that the *miai* looked to be heavily weighted towards the prospective groom's family – his younger brother, as well as his parents, intended to be present. It would be perfectly acceptable, he gave me to understand, if we were to bring a relative or close friend to give Noriko additional support. But of course, with Setsuko so far away, there was no one we could properly ask to attend such an occasion. And it may well have been this feeling that we would somehow be at a disadvantage at the *miai*, together with our unhappiness with the venue, that caused Noriko to be more tense about the matter than she might otherwise have been. In any case, the weeks leading up to the *miai* were difficult ones.

Often, she would come home from her office and immediately make some remark like: 'What have you been doing all day, Father? Just moping around as usual, I expect.' Far from 'moping around', as it happened, I would have been busy in my efforts to secure a good outcome to the marriage negotiations. But because at that time I believed it important not to worry her with details of how matters were proceeding, I would talk only vaguely concerning my day, thus allowing her to continue with her insinuations. In retrospect, I see that our not openly discussing certain matters may well have made Noriko all the more tense, and a franker approach on my part may well have prevented many of the unpleasant exchanges that took place between us around that time.

I recall one afternoon, for instance, Noriko arriving home as I was pruning some shrubs out in the garden. She had greeted me from the veranda in a perfectly civil way, before disappearing again into the house. Then a few minutes later I was sitting on the veranda, looking out at the garden to assess the effect of my work, when Noriko, now changed into a kimono, appeared again with some tea. She put the tray down between us and seated herself. It was, as I recall, one of the last of those splendid autumn afternoons we had last year, and a tender light was falling across the foliage. Following my gaze, she said:

'Father, why have you cut the bamboo like that? It looks unbalanced now.'

'Unbalanced? Do you think so? I think it looks balanced enough. You see, you have to take into account where the younger shoots are dominant.'

'Father tends to meddle too much. I think he's going to ruin that bush too.'

'Ruin that bush too?' I turned towards my daughter. 'Whatever do you mean? You're saying I've ruined others?'

'The azaleas have never regained their looks. That's what comes of Father having so much time on his hands. He ends up meddling where it's not required.'

'Excuse me, Noriko, I don't quite see your point. You're saying the azaleas are unbalanced too?'

Noriko looked at the garden again and gave a sigh. 'You should have left things as they were.'

'I'm sorry, Noriko, but to my eyes, both the bamboo and the azaleas are much improved. I'm afraid I don't see your "unbalanced" aspect at all.'

'Well then, Father must be going blind. Or perhaps it's just poor taste.'

'Poor taste? Now that's curious. You know, Noriko, people have not on the whole associated poor taste with my name.'

'Well, to my eyes, Father,' she said tiredly, 'the bamboo is unbalanced. And you've spoiled the way the tree hangs over it too.'

For a moment, I sat gazing at the garden in silence. 'Yes,' I said, eventually, and gave a nod. 'I suppose you might see it that way, Noriko. You never did have an artistic instinct. Neither you nor Setsuko. Kenji was another matter, but you girls took after your mother. In fact, I remember your mother used to make just such misguided comments.'

'Is Father such an authority on how to cut shrubs? I didn't realize that. I'm sorry.'

'I didn't claim to be an authority. It's simply that I'm a little surprised to be accused of poor taste. It's an unusual accusation in my own case, that's all.'

'Very well, Father, I'm sure it's all a matter of opinion.'

'Your mother was rather like you, Noriko. She had no bones about saying whatever came into her head. It's quite honest, I suppose.'

'I'm sure Father knows best about such things. That's beyond dispute, no doubt.'

'I remember, Noriko, your mother would sometimes even make her comments while I was painting. She would try to make some point and make me laugh. Then she'd laugh, too, and concede she knew little about such things.'

'So Father was always right about his paintings too, I suppose.'

'Noriko, this is a pointless discussion. Besides, if you don't like what I've done in the garden, you're welcome to go out there and do what you like to set things right.'

'That's very kind of Father. But when do you suggest I do it? I don't have all day long as Father does.'

'What do you mean, Noriko? I've had a busy day.' I glared at her for a moment, but she went on looking at the garden, a weary expression on her face. I turned away and gave a sigh. 'But this is a pointless discussion. Your mother at least could say such things and we would laugh together.'

At such moments, it was indeed tempting to point out to her the extent to which I was in fact exerting myself on her behalf. Had I done so, my daughter would no doubt have been surprised – and, I dare say, ashamed at her behaviour towards me. That very day, for instance, I had actually been to the Yanagawa district, where I had discovered Kuroda was now living.

It had not, in the end, been a difficult task to discover Kuroda's whereabouts. The art professor at Uemachi College, once I had assured him of my good intentions, had given me not only the address, but an account of what had been happening to my former pupil over these past years. Kuroda, it seemed, had not fared at all badly since his release at the end of the war. Such are the ways of this world that his years in prison gave him strong credentials, and certain groups had made a point of welcoming him and seeing to his needs. He had thus experienced little difficulty finding work – mainly small tutoring jobs – or the materials to recommence his own painting. Then, towards the early part of last summer, he had been given the post of art teacher at Uemachi College.

Now, it may seem somewhat perverse of me to say so, but I was pleased – and indeed rather proud – to hear Kuroda's career was progressing well. But then it is only natural after all that his former teacher should continue to take pride in such things, even if circumstances have caused teacher and pupil to become estranged.

Kuroda did not live in a good quarter. I walked for some time through little alleys filled with dilapidated lodging houses before coming to a concrete square resembling the forecourt of a factory. Indeed, across the square, I could see some trucks had been parked, and farther on, behind a mesh fence, a bulldozer was churning up the ground. I recall I was standing watching the bulldozer for some moments before realizing the large new building above me was in fact Kuroda's apartment block.

I climbed to the second floor, where two small boys were riding a tricycle up and down the corridor, and searched out Kuroda's door. My first ring was not answered, but I was by then firmly resolved to go ahead with the encounter and rang again.

A fresh-faced young man of around twenty opened the door.

'I'm very sorry' – he spoke very earnestly – 'but Mr Kuroda isn't home at present. I wonder, sir, are you perhaps a work associate?'

'In a manner of speaking. There were a few matters I wished to discuss with Mr Kuroda.'

'In that case, perhaps you'd be so good as to come in and wait. I'm sure Mr Kuroda will not be gone long, and he would very much regret it if he were to miss you.'

'But I don't wish to put you to any bother.'

'Not at all, sir. Please, please come in.'

The apartment was small, and like many of these modern affairs, had no entryway as such, the tatami starting a little way inside the front door with only a shallow step up. There was a tidy look to the place, and a number of paintings and hangings adorned the walls. Plenty of sunlight came into the apartment through the large windows, which I could see opened on to a narrow balcony. The noise of the bulldozer could be heard coming from outside.

'I hope you were not in a hurry, sir,' the young man said, placing a cushion for me. 'But Mr Kuroda would never forgive me if he returned to learn I had let you go. Please allow me to make you some tea.'

'How very kind,' I said, seating myself. 'You are a student of Mr Kuroda's?'

The young man gave a small laugh. 'Mr Kuroda is kind enough to refer to me as his protégé, although I am myself doubtful if I am worthy of such a title. My name is Enchi. Mr Kuroda used to tutor me, and now, despite his heavy commitments at his college, he most generously continues to take an interest in my work.'

'Is that so?'

From outside came the noise of the bulldozer at work. For a moment or two, the young man hovered awkwardly, then excused himself, saying: 'Please, I will prepare some tea.'

A few minutes later, when he reappeared, I pointed to a painting on the wall, saying: 'Mr Kuroda's style is quite unmistakable.'

At this, the young man gave a laugh and looked awkwardly towards the painting, the tea tray still in his hands. Then he said:

'I'm afraid that painting is far from Mr Kuroda's standards, sir.'

'It isn't Mr Kuroda's work?'

'I'm afraid, sir, that is one of my own efforts. My teacher has been so good as to deem it worthy of display.'

'Really? Well, well.'

I went on gazing up at the painting. The young man put the tray down on a low table near me, and seated himself.

'Really, that is your own work? Well, I must say you have much talent. Much talent indeed.'

He gave another embarrassed laugh. 'I'm very fortunate in having Mr Kuroda for a teacher. But I fear I still have much to learn.'

'And I was so sure it was an example of Mr Kuroda's own

work. The brush strokes have that quality to them.'

The young man was fussing rather clumsily with the teapot, as though unsure how to proceed. I watched him lift up the lid to peer inside.

'Mr Kuroda is always telling me,' he said, 'I should try and paint in a style more distinctly my own. But I find so much to admire in Mr Kuroda's ways, I can hardly help mimicking him.'

'It's no bad thing to mimic one's teacher for a while. One learns a lot that way. But all in good time, you'll develop your own ideas and techniques, for you're undoubtedly a young man of much talent. Yes, I'm sure you have a most promising future. It's no wonder Mr Kuroda takes an interest in you.'

'I cannot begin to tell you, sir, what I owe to Mr Kuroda. Why, as you can see, I am now even lodging here in his apartment. I have been here for almost two weeks. I was thrown out of my previous lodgings, and Mr Kuroda came to my rescue. It is impossible to tell you, sir, all he has done for me.'

'You say you were thrown out of your lodgings?'

'I assure you, sir,' he said, with a small laugh, 'I paid my rent. But you see, as much as I tried, I could not avoid getting paint on the tatami, and eventually the landlord threw me out.'

We both laughed at this. Then I said:

'I'm sorry, I don't mean to be unsympathetic. It's just that I remember just such problems myself when I was starting out. But you'll soon acquire the right conditions to work if you persevere, I assure you.'

We both laughed again.

'You're very encouraging, sir,' the young man said, and began to pour the tea. 'I don't suppose Mr Kuroda will be long now. I beg you not to hurry away. Mr Kuroda will be most glad for the opportunity to thank you for all you have done.'

I looked at him in surprise. 'You think Mr Kuroda wishes to thank me?'

'Excuse me, sir, but I was assuming you are from the Cordon Society.'

'The Cordon Society? I'm sorry, what is that?'

The young man glanced towards me, some of his earlier awkwardness returning. 'I'm sorry, sir, it's my mistake. I assumed you were from the Cordon Society.'

'I'm afraid I'm not. I'm simply an old acquaintance of Mr Kuroda's.'

'I see. An old colleague?'

'Indeed. I suppose you could say that.' I gazed up again at the young man's painting on the wall. 'Yes, indeed,' I said. 'Very talented. Very talented indeed.' I had become aware that the young man was now looking at me carefully. Eventually, he said:

'I'm sorry, sir, but may I ask your name?'

'I'm sorry, you must think me most rude. My name is Ono.'

'I see.'

The young man rose to his feet and went over to the window. For a moment or two, I watched the steam rising from the two cups on the table.

'Will Mr Kuroda be long now?' I asked, eventually.

At first, I did not think the young man was going to reply. But then he said, without turning from the window: 'Perhaps if he has not returned soon, you should not detain yourself further from your other business.'

'If you don't mind, I'll wait a little longer, now that I've made the journey out here.'

'I will inform Mr Kuroda of your visit. Perhaps he will write to you.'

Out in the corridor, the children seemed to be banging their tricycle against the wall not far from us and shouting at each other. It struck me then how much like a sulking child the young man at the window looked.

'Forgive me for saying this, Mr Enchi,' I said. 'But you are very young. Indeed, you could only have been a boy when Mr Kuroda and I first knew each other. I would ask you not to jump to conclusions about matters of which you do not know the full details.'

'The full details?' he said, turning to me. 'Excuse me, sir, but are you yourself aware of the full details? Do you know what he suffered?'

'Most things are more complicated than they appear, Mr Enchi. Young men of your generation tend to see things far too simply. In any case, there seems little point in the two of us debating such matters at this moment. I will, if you don't mind, wait for Mr Kuroda.'

'I would suggest, sir, you delay yourself no further from your other business. I will inform Mr Kuroda when he returns.' Until this point, the young man had managed to maintain a polite tone in his voice, but now he seemed to lose his self-control. 'Frankly, sir, I am amazed at your nerve. To come here as though you were simply a friendly visitor.'

'But I am a friendly visitor. And if I may say so, I think it is for Mr Kuroda to decide whether or not he wishes to receive me as such.'

'Sir, I have come to know Mr Kuroda well, and in my judgement it is best you leave. He will not wish to see you.'

I gave a sigh and rose to my feet. The young man was again looking out of the window. But as I was removing my hat from the coat stand, he turned to me once more. 'The full details, Mr Ono,' he said, and his voice had a strange kind of composure. 'It is clearly you who are ignorant of the full details. Or else how would you dare come here like this? For instance, sir, I take it you never knew about Mr Kuroda's shoulder? He was in great pain, but the warders conveniently forgot to report the injury and it was not attended to until the end of the war. But of course, they remembered it well enough whenever they decided to give him another beating. Traitor. That's what they called him. Traitor. Every minute of every day. But now we all know who the real traitors were.'

113

I finished lacing my shoes and started for the door.

'You're too young, Mr Enchi, to know about this world and its complications.'

'We all know now who the real traitors were. And many of them are still walking free.'

'You will tell Mr Kuroda I was here? Perhaps he will be so good as to write to me. Good day, Mr Enchi.'

Naturally, I did not allow the young man's words to upset me unduly, but in the light of Noriko's marriage negotiations, the possibility that Kuroda was as hostile to my memory as Enchi had suggested was indeed a disturbing one. It was, in any case, my duty as a father to press on with the matter, unpleasant though it was, and on returning home that afternoon, I composed a letter to Kuroda, expressing my desire that we should meet again, particularly since I had a matter of some delicacy and importance to discuss with him. The tone of my letter had been friendly and conciliatory, and so I was disappointed by the cold and offensively brief reply I received a few days later.

'I have no reason to believe a meeting between us would produce anything of value,' my former pupil had written. 'I thank you for your courtesy in calling the other day, but I feel I should not trouble you further to fulfil such obligations.'

This matter with Kuroda did, I confess, cast something of a shadow over my mood; it certainly marred my optimism concerning Noriko's negotiations. And though, as I have said, I kept from her the details of my attempts to meet with Kuroda, my daughter undoubtedly sensed the matter had not been resolved satisfactorily, and this no doubt contributed to her anxiety.

On the actual day of the *miai* itself, my daughter seemed so tense, I became concerned as to the impression she would make that evening in front of the Saitos – who were themselves bound to display a smooth and relaxed assurance. Towards the latter part of the afternoon, I felt it would be prudent to try and lighten Noriko's mood somewhat, and this was the impulse behind my remarking to her as she passed through the dining room where I was sat reading:

'It's astonishing, Noriko, how you can spend the whole day doing nothing but preparing your appearance. You'd think this was the marriage ceremony itself.'

'It's just like Father to mock then not be properly ready himself,' she snapped back.

'I'll only need a little time to be ready,' I said, with a laugh. 'Quite extraordinary, your taking the whole day like this.'

'That's Father's trouble. He's too proud to prepare properly for these things.'

I looked up at her in astonishment. 'What do you mean, "too proud"? What are you suggesting, Noriko?'

My daughter turned away, adjusting her hairclasp.

'Noriko, what do you mean, "too proud"? What are you suggesting?'

'If Father doesn't want to make a fuss over something as trivial as my future, then that's quite understandable. After all, Father hasn't even finished his newspaper yet.'

'But you're changing your tack now. You were saying something about my being "too proud". Why don't you say more about it?'

'I just hope Father's presentable when the time comes,' she said, and went purposefully out of the room.

On that occasion, as often during those difficult days, I was obliged to reflect on the marked contrast of Noriko's attitude with that she had displayed the previous year, during the negotiations with the Miyake family. Then, she had been relaxed almost to the point of complacency; but of course, she had known Jiro Miyake well; I dare say she had been confident the two of them would marry, and had regarded the discussions between families as nothing more than cumbersome formalities. No doubt the shock she subsequently received was a bitter one, but it seems to me unnecessary for her to have made insinuations such as she did that afternoon. In any case, that little altercation hardly helped to put us in the right frame of mind for a *miai*, and in all likelihood contributed to what took place that evening at the Kasuga Park Hotel.

For many years, the Kasuga Park Hotel had been amongst the most pleasant of the Western-style hotels in the city; these days, though, the management has taken to decorating the rooms in a somewhat vulgar manner – intended, no doubt, to strike the American clientele with whom the place is popular as being charmingly 'Japanese'. For all that, the room Mr Kyo had booked was pleasing enough, its main feature being the view from the wide bay windows down the west slope of Kasuga Hill, the lights of the city visible far below us. Otherwise, the room was dominated by a large circular table and high-backed chairs, and a painting on one wall which I recognized to be by Matsumoto, an artist I had known slightly before the war.

It may well be that the tension of the occasion made me drink a little more quickly than I intended, for my memories of the evening are not as clear as they might be. I do remember forming immediately a favourable impression of Taro Saito, the young man I was being asked to consider for a son-in-law. Not only did he seem an intelligent, responsible sort, he possessed all the assured grace and manners I admired in his father. Indeed, observing the unworried, yet highly courteous way Taro Saito received myself and Noriko as we first arrived, I was reminded of another young man who had impressed me in a parallel situation some years earlier – that is to say, Suichi at Setsuko's *miai* at what was in those days the Imperial Inn. And for a moment, I considered the possibility that Taro Saito's courtesy and good-naturedness would fade with time as surely as Suichi's has done. But then, of course, it is to be hoped that Taro Saito will never have to endure the embittering experiences Suichi is said to have done.

As for Dr Saito himself, he seemed as commanding a presence as ever. Despite our never having been properly introduced prior to that evening, Dr Saito and I had in fact been acquainted for some years, having taken to greeting one another in the street out of mutual recognition of our respective reputations. His wife, a handsome woman in her fifties, I had likewise exchanged greetings with, but little else; I could see she was, like her husband, someone of considerable poise, confident of handling any awkward situation that might arise. The only member of the Saito family who did not impress me was the younger son – Mitsuo – whom I guessed to be in his early twenties.

Now that I think back to that evening, I am sure my suspicions about young Mitsuo were aroused as soon as I saw him. I am still uncertain as to what first set off a warning – perhaps it was that he reminded me of young Enchi whom I had encountered in Kuroda's apartment. In any case, as we began to eat, I found myself becoming increasingly confirmed in these suspicions. Although at this point Mitsuo was behaving with all due decorum, there was something in the way I would catch him looking at me, or about the way he would pass a bowl to me across the table, that made me sense his hostility and accusation.

And then, after we had been eating for several minutes, I was struck by a sudden thought; that Mitsuo's attitude was not in fact any different from that of the rest of his family – it was simply that he was not as skilled in disguising it. From then on, I took to glancing over at Mitsuo, as though he were the clearest indicator of what the Saitos were really thinking. However, because he was sitting at some distance across the table, and because Mr Kyo, next to him, appeared to be engaging him in prolonged conversation, I did not have any significant exchanges with Mitsuo at that stage of the proceedings.

'We hear you're fond of playing the piano, Miss Noriko,' I remember Mrs Saito remarking at one point.

Noriko gave a small laugh and said: 'I don't practise nearly enough.'

'I used to play when I was younger,' said Mrs Saito. 'But now I too am out of practice. We women are given so little time for such pursuits, don't you think?'

'Indeed,' my daughter said, rather nervously.

'I have very poor appreciation of music myself,' Taro Saito put in, gazing unflinchingly at Noriko. 'In fact, my mother always accuses me of being tone-deaf. As a result, I have no confidence in my own taste, and I'm obliged to consult her about which composers to admire.'

'What nonsense,' said Mrs Saito.

'You know, Miss Noriko,' Taro went on, 'I once acquired a set of recordings of a Bach piano concerto. I was very fond of it, but my mother was forever criticizing it and chastising my poor taste. Naturally my opinions stood little chance against the likes of Mother here. Consequently I now hardly listen to Bach. But perhaps you could come to my rescue, Miss Noriko. Aren't you fond of Bach?'

'Bach?' For a second, my daughter looked at a loss. Then she smiled and said: 'Yes, indeed. Very much so.'

'Ah,' Taro Saito said triumphantly, 'now Mother will need to reconsider things.'

'My son is talking nonsense, Miss Noriko. I've never criticized Bach's work as a whole. But tell me, don't you agree Chopin is more eloquent so far as the piano is concerned?'

'Indeed,' said Noriko.

Such stiff responses typified my daughter's performance for much of the earlier part of the evening. This was not, I might say, altogether unexpected. When amongst family, or in the company of close friends, Noriko is in the habit of adopting her somewhat flippant manner of address, and often achieves a wit and eloquence of sorts; but in more formal settings, I have often known her to have difficulty finding an appropriate tone, thus giving the impression she is a timid young woman. That this was precisely what was occurring on this of all occasions was reason for concern; for it seemed to me clear – and Mrs Saito's own high profile appeared to confirm this – the Saitos were not the old-fashioned sort of family who preferred their female members to be silent and demure. I had in fact anticipated this, and in our preparations for the *miai*, had stressed my opinion that Noriko should as far as appropriate emphasize her lively, intelligent qualities. My daughter had been in full agreement with such a strategy, and indeed, had declared so determinedly her intention to behave in a frank and natural way, I had even feared she would go too far and outrage the proceedings. So, as I watched her struggling to produce simple, compliant replies to the Saitos' promptings, her gaze rarely leaving her bowl, I could imagine the frustration Noriko was experiencing.

Noriko's problems aside, however, talk seemed to flow easily around the table. Dr Saito in particular proved so expert at generating a relaxed atmosphere, that, had it not been for my awareness of young Mitsuo's gaze on me, I might well have forgotten the gravity of the occasion and lowered my guard. At one point during the meal, I can recall Dr Saito leaning back comfortably in his chair, saying:

'It seems there were more demonstrations in the city centre today. You know, Mr Ono, I was on the tram this afternoon and a man got in with a large bruise over his forehead. He sat next to me, so naturally I asked him if he was all right and advised him to visit the clinic. But you know, it turned out he had just been to a doctor, and he was now determined to rejoin his companions in the demonstrations. What do you make of that, Mr Ono?'

Dr Saito had spoken casually enough, but I got for a moment the impression that the whole table – Noriko included – had stopped eating to hear my reply. It is quite possible, of course, that I imagined this; but then I do recall quite distinctly that when I threw a glance towards young Mitsuo, he was watching me with a peculiar intensity.

'It's regrettable indeed,' I said, 'that people are getting hurt. No doubt feelings are running high.'

'I'm sure you're right, Mr Ono,' Mrs Saito put in. 'Feelings may well be running high, but people seem to be going too far now. So many getting injured. But my husband here claims it's all for the good. I really don't understand what he means.'

I expected Dr Saito to react to this, but instead there was another pause during which attention seemed once more to focus in my direction.

'It is, as you say,' I remarked, 'a great pity so many have been injured.'

'My wife is misrepresenting me as usual, Mr Ono,' Dr Saito said. 'I never claimed all this fighting was a good thing. But I've been trying to convince my wife there's more to these things than simply people getting injured. Of course, one doesn't want to see people hurt. But the underlying spirit – that people feel the need to express their views openly and strongly – now that's a healthy thing, don't you think so, Mr Ono?'

Perhaps I hesitated for a moment; in any case, Taro Saito spoke before I could reply.

'But surely, Father, things are getting out of hand now. Democracy is a fine thing, but it doesn't mean citizens have a right to run riot whenever they disagree with something. In this respect, we Japanese have been shown to be like children. We've yet to learn how to handle the responsibility of democracy.'

'Here's an unusual case,' Dr Saito said, laughing. 'It seems on this question at least, it's the father who's far more liberal than the son. Taro may be right. At this moment, our country is like a young boy learning to walk and run. But I say the underlying spirit is healthy. It's like watching a growing boy running and grazing his knee. One doesn't wish to prevent him and keep him locked indoors. Don't you think so, Mr Ono? Or am I being too liberal, as my wife and my son insist?'

Perhaps again I was mistaken – for as I say, I was drinking a little faster than I had intended – but there seemed to me a curious lack of disharmony about the Saito's supposed difference of views. Meanwhile, young Mitsuo, I noticed, was once more watching me.

'Indeed,' I said. 'I hope no more people are injured.'

I believe at this point Taro Saito changed the subject by asking Noriko her opinion on one of the city's recently opened department stores, and for a while the conversation reverted to smaller topics.

These occasions are not, of course, easy for any prospective bride – it seems unfair to ask a young woman to make judgements so crucial to her future happiness while under such scrutiny herself – but I must admit I had not expected Noriko to take the tension quite so badly. As the evening progressed, her confidence seemed to wane further and further, until she seemed unable to say little more than 'yes' or 'no'. Taro Saito, I could see, was doing his best to get Noriko to relax, but the occasion demanded he should not appear overly persistent, and time and again, his attempts to start a humorous exchange would end in awkward silences. As I watched my daughter's distress, I was struck again by the contrast of the proceedings with the *miai* the previous year. Setsuko, down on one of her visits then, had been present to give her sister support, but Noriko had seemed in little need of it that night. Indeed, I could recall my irritation at the way Noriko and Jiro Miyake had continued to exchange mischievous glances across the table, as though to mock the formality of the occasion.

'You remember, Mr Ono,' Dr Saito said, 'the last time we met, we discovered we had a mutual acquaintance. A Mr Kuroda.'

We were by this time nearing the end of the meal.

'Ah yes, indeed,' I said.

'My son here' – Dr Saito indicated young Mitsuo with whom I had so far exchanged barely a word – 'is presently studying at Uemachi College, where, of course, Mr Kuroda is now teaching.'

'Is that so?' I turned to the young man. 'So you know Mr Kuroda well?'

'Not well,' the young man said. 'Regrettably, I have no ability in the arts, and my contact with the art professors is limited.'

'But Mr Kuroda is well spoken of, isn't he, Mitsuo?' Dr Saito put in.

'He is indeed.'

'Mr Ono here was a close acquaintance of Mr Kuroda once. Did you know that?'

'Yes, I'd heard,' Mitsuo said.

At this point, Taro Saito changed the subject again by saying:

'You know, Miss Noriko, I've always had a theory about my poor ear for music. When I was a child, my parents never kept the piano tuned. Every day, throughout my most formative years, Miss Noriko, I was obliged to listen to Mother here practising on an out-of-tune piano. It's quite possible, don't you think, this is behind all my troubles?'

'Yes,' Noriko said, and looked back down at her food.

'There. I always maintained it was Mother's fault. And she's constantly chastised me all these years for having a bad ear. I've been most unfairly treated, wouldn't you say, Miss Noriko?'

Noriko smiled, but said nothing.

Around this point, evidently, Mr Kyo, who had thus far kept in the background, began to tell one of his comic anecdotes. According at least to Noriko's account of things, he was still in the midst of his story when I interrupted by turning to young Mitsuo Saito and saying:

'Mr Kuroda has no doubt spoken to you about me.'

Mitsuo looked up with a puzzled expression.

'Spoken about you, sir?' he said, hesitantly. 'I'm sure he often mentions you, but I'm afraid I'm not well acquainted with Mr Kuroda and consequently . . .' He trailed off, and looked towards his parents for help.

'I'm sure,' Dr Saito said, in what struck me as a rather deliberate voice, 'Mr Kuroda remembers Mr Ono well enough.'

'I do not think,' I said, looking at Mitsuo again, 'that Mr Kuroda would have a particularly high opinion of me.'

The young man turned awkwardly once more towards his parents. This time, it was Mrs Saito who said:

'On the contrary, I'm sure he would have the highest opinion of you, Mr Ono.'

'There are some, Mrs Saito,' I said, perhaps a little loudly, 'who believe my career to have been a negative influence. An influence now best erased and forgotten. I am not unaware of this viewpoint. Mr Kuroda, I would think, is one who would hold it.'

'Is that so?' Perhaps I was mistaken about this, but I thought Dr Saito was watching me rather like a teacher waiting for a pupil to go on with a lesson he has learnt by heart.

'Indeed. And as for myself, I am now quite prepared to accept the validity of such an opinion.'

'I'm sure you're being unfair on yourself, Mr Ono,' Taro Saito began to say, but I quickly went on:

'There are some who would say it is people like myself who are responsible for the terrible things that happened to this nation of ours. As far as I am concerned, I freely admit I made many mistakes. I accept that much of what I did was ultimately harmful to our nation, that mine was part of an influence that resulted in untold suffering for our own people. I admit this. You see, Dr Saito, I admit this quite readily.'

Dr Saito leaned forward, a puzzled expression on his face.

'Forgive me, Mr Ono,' he said. 'You're saying you are unhappy about the work you did? With your paintings?'

'My paintings. My teachings. As you see, Dr Saito, I admit this quite readily. All I can say is that at the time I acted in good faith. I believed in all sincerity I was achieving good for my fellow countrymen. But as you see, I am not now afraid to admit I was mistaken.'

'I'm sure you're too harsh on yourself, Mr Ono,' Taro Saito said cheerfully. Then turning to Noriko, he said: 'Tell me, Miss Noriko, is your father always so strict with himself?'

Noriko, I realized, had been staring at me in astonishment. Perhaps as a result of this, she was taken off guard by Taro, and her customary flippancy came to her lips for the first time that evening.

'Father's not strict at all. It's me that has to be strict with him. Otherwise he'd never be up for breakfast.'

'Is that so?' Taro Saito said, delighted to have drawn a less formal response from Noriko. 'My father is also a late riser. They say older people sleep less than we do, but from our experience this seems quite incorrect.'

Noriko laughed and said: 'I think it's just fathers. I'm sure Mrs Saito has no trouble getting up.'

'A fine thing,' Dr Saito remarked to me. 'They're making fun of us and we're not even out of the room.'

I would not wish to claim that the whole engagement had hung in the balance until that point, but it is certainly my feeling that that was when the *miai* turned from being an awkward, potentially disastrous one into a successful evening. We went on talking and drinking sake for a good while after the meal, and by the time taxis were called, there was a clear feeling that we had all got on well. Most crucially, although they had kept an appropriate distance, it was obvious Taro Saito and Noriko had taken to one another.

Of course, I do not pretend certain moments of that evening were not painful for me; nor do I claim I would so easily have made the sort of declaration I did concerning the past had circumstances not impressed upon me the prudence of doing so. Having said this, I must say I find it hard to understand how any man who values his self-respect would wish for long to avoid responsibility for his past deeds; it may not always be an easy thing, but there is certainly a satisfaction and dignity to be gained in coming to terms with the mistakes one has made in the course of one's life. In any case, there is surely no great shame in mistakes made in the best of faith. It is surely a thing far more shameful to be unable or unwilling to acknowledge them.

Consider Shintaro, for instance – who appears, incidentally, to have secured the teaching post he was so coveting. Shintaro would in my view be a happier man today if he had the courage and honesty to accept what he did in the past. It is, I suppose, possible that the cold reaction he received from me that afternoon just after New Year may have persuaded him to change tack in dealing with his committee over the matter of his China crisis posters. But my guess is that Shintaro persisted with his small hypocrisies in pursuit of his goal. Indeed, I have come to believe now that there has always been a cunning, underhand side to Shintaro's nature, which I had not really noticed in the past.

'You know, Obasan,' I said to Mrs Kawakami when I was down there one evening not so long ago, 'I rather suspect Shintaro was never quite the unworldly sort he would have us believe. That's just his way of gaining an advantage over people and getting things to go his way. People like Shintaro, if they don't want to do something, they pretend they're helplessly lost about it and they're forgiven everything.'

'Really, Sensei.' Mrs Kawakami gave me a disapproving look, understandably reluctant to think ill of someone who had for so long been her best customer.

'For instance, Obasan,' I went on, 'think how cleverly he avoided the war. While others were losing so much, Shintaro just went on working in that little studio of his as though nothing was happening.'

'But Sensei, Shintaro-san has a bad leg . . .'

'Bad leg or not, everyone was being called up. Of course, they found him in the end, but then the war was over within days. You know, Obasan, Shintaro told me once he lost two working weeks on account of the war. That's what the war cost Shintaro. Believe me, Obasan, there's far more to our old friend beneath his childish exterior.'

'Well, in any case,' Mrs Kawakami said tiredly, 'it looks as though he won't be returning here any more now.'

'Indeed, Obasan. It seems you've lost him for good.'

Mrs Kawakami, a cigarette burning in her hand, leaned on her edge of the counter and cast an eye around her little bar. We were as usual alone in the place. The early evening sun was coming in through the mosquito nets on the windows, making the room look more dusty and older than it does once darkness has set in and Mrs Kawakami's lamps are illuminating it. Outside, the men were still working. For the past hour, the sound of hammering had been echoing in from somewhere, and a truck starting or a burst of drilling would frequently cause the whole place to shake. And as I followed Mrs Kawakami's glance around the room that summer's evening, I was struck by the thought of how small, shabby and out of place her little bar would seem amidst the large concrete buildings the city corporation was even at that moment erecting around us. And I said to Mrs Kawakami:

'You know, Obasan, you really must think seriously about accepting this offer and moving elsewhere now. It's a great opportunity.'

'But I've been here so long,' she said, and waved a hand to clear the smoke from her cigarette.

'You could open a fine new place, Obasan. In the Kitabashi district, or even in Honcho. You can be sure I'll drop in whenever I'm passing by.'

Mrs Kawakami was quiet for a moment, as though listening for something amidst the sounds the workmen were making outside. Then a smile spread over her face and she said: 'This was such a splendid district once. You remember, Sensei?'

I returned her smile, but did not say anything. Of course, the old district had been fine. We had all enjoyed ourselves and the spirit that had pervaded the bantering and those arguments had never been less than sincere. But then perhaps that same spirit had not always been for the best. Like many things now, it is perhaps as well that that little world has passed away and will not be returning. I was tempted to say as much to Mrs Kawakami that evening, but decided it would be tactless to do so. For clearly, the old district was dear to her heart – much of her life and energy had been invested in it – and one can surely understand her reluctance to accept it has gone for ever.

NOVEMBER, 1949

My recollection of the first time I ever met Dr Saito remains quite vivid, and I am thus confident enough of its accuracy. It must have been all of sixteen years ago now, on the day after I moved into my house. I recall it being a bright summer's day, and I was outside adjusting the fence, or perhaps fixing something to the gateway, and exchanging greetings with those of my new neighbours who passed by. Then at one point, after my back had been turned to the path for some time, I became aware that someone was standing behind me, apparently to watch me work. I turned to find a man of around my own age studying with interest my newly inscribed name on the gatepost.

'So you are Mr Ono,' he remarked. 'Well now, this is a real honour. A real honour to have someone of your stature here in our neighbourhood. I am myself, you see, involved in the world of fine art. My name is Saito, from the Imperial City University.'

'Dr Saito? Why, this is a great privilege. I have heard much about you, sir.'

I believe we went on talking for several moments there outside my gateway, and I am sure I am not mistaken in recalling that Dr Saito, on that same occasion, made several more references to my work and career. And before he went on his way down the hill, I remember his repeating words to the effect of: 'A great honour to have an artist of your stature in our neighbourhood, Mr Ono.'

Thereafter, Dr Saito and I always greeted each other respectfully whenever we chanced to meet. It is true, I suppose, that after that initial encounter – until recent events gave us cause for greater intimacy – we rarely stopped for prolonged conversations. But my memory of that first meeting, and of Dr Saito recognizing my name on the gatepost, is sufficiently clear for me to assert with some confidence that my elder daughter, Setsuko, was quite mistaken in at least some of the things she tried to imply last month. It is hardly possible, for instance, that Dr Saito had no idea who I was until the marriage negotiations last year obliged him to find out.

Because her visit this year was so brief, and because she spent it staying at Noriko and Taro's new home in the Izumimachi district, my walk with Setsuko that morning through Kawabe Park was really my only chance to speak properly with her. It is not surprising then that I should be turning that conversation over in my mind for some time afterwards, and I do not think it unreasonable that I now find myself becoming increasingly irritated by certain things she said to me that day.

At the time, however, I could not have been dwelling too deeply on Setsuko's words, for I recall being in a good enough mood, happy to be in my daughter's company again, and enjoying walking through Kawabe Park, which I had not done for a while. This was just over a month ago, when as you will recall, the days were still sunny, though the leaves were already falling. Setsuko and I were making our way down the wide avenue of trees that runs through the middle of the park, and because we were well ahead of the time we had agreed to meet Noriko and Ichiro beside the statue of the Emperor Taisho, we were walking at an easy pace, stopping every now and then to admire the autumn scenery.

Perhaps you will agree with me that Kawabe Park is the most rewarding of the city parks; certainly after one has been walking around those crowded little streets of the Kawabe district for a time, it is most refreshing to find oneself in one of those spacious long avenues hung over with trees. But if you are new to this city, and unfamiliar with the history of

Kawabe Park, I should perhaps explain here why the park has always held a special interest for me.

Here and there around the park, you will no doubt recall passing certain isolated patches of grass, none larger than a school yard, visible through the trees as you walk down any of those avenues. It is as though those who planned the park had become confused and abandoned some scheme or other half-completed. This, in fact, was more or less the case. Some years ago, Akira Sugimura – he whose house I had bought shortly after his death – had the most ambitious of plans concerning Kawabe Park. I realize Akira Sugimura's name is rarely heard these days, but let me point out that not so long ago he was unquestionably one of the most influential men in the city. At one stage, so I heard, he possessed four houses, and it was hardly possible to walk around this city for long before stumbling across some enterprise or other owned by or connected heavily with Sugimura. Then, around 1920 or 1921, at the peak of his success, Sugimura decided to gamble much of his wealth and capital on a project that would allow him to leave his mark for ever on this city and its people. He planned to convert Kawabe Park – which was then a rather drab neglected place – into the focus of the city's culture. Not only would the grounds be enlarged to contain more natural areas for people to relax, the park was to become the site for several glittering cultural centres – a museum of natural science; a new kabuki theatre for the Takahashi school, who had recently lost their venue in Shirahama Street through fire; a European-style concert hall; and also, somewhat eccentrically, a cemetery for the city's cats and dogs. I cannot remember what else he planned, but there was no mistaking the sweeping ambition of the scheme. Sugimura hoped not only to transform the Kawabe district, but the whole cultural balance of the city, bringing a new emphasis to the northern side of the river. It was, as I have said, nothing less than the attempt of one man to stamp his mark for ever on the character of the city.

133

Work on the park was well underway, it seems, when the scheme ran into terrible financial difficulties. I am not clear on the details of the affair, but the result was that Sugimura's 'cultural centres' were never built. Sugimura himself lost a great deal of money and never again regained his old influence. After the war, Kawabe Park came under the direct control of the city authorities who built the avenues of trees. All that remain today of Sugimura's schemes are those oddly empty patches of grass where his museums and theatres would have stood.

I may have said before that my dealings with Sugimura's family after his death – on the occasion of my buying the last of his houses – were not of the kind to make me particularly well disposed to the man's memory. Nevertheless, whenever I find myself wandering around Kawabe Park these days, I start to think of Sugimura and his schemes, and I confess I am beginning to feel a certain admiration for the man. For indeed, a man who aspires to rise above the mediocre, to be something more than ordinary, surely deserves admiration, even if in the end he fails and loses a fortune on account of his ambitions. It is my belief, furthermore, that Sugimura did not die an unhappy man. For his failure was quite unlike the undignified failures of most ordinary lives, and a man like Sugimura would have known this. If one has failed only where others have not had the courage or will to try, there is a consolation – indeed, a deep satisfaction – to be gained from this observation when looking back over one's life.

But it was not my intention to dwell on Sugimura. As I say, I was by and large enjoying my walk through Kawabe Park with Setsuko that day, notwithstanding certain of her remarks – whose significance I did not fully grasp until I reflected on them some time later. In any case, our conversation was brought to an end by the fact that in the middle of our path only a short distance ahead loomed the statue of the Emperor Taisho where we had arranged to meet Noriko and Ichiro. I was casting my gaze towards the benches that circled the statue when I heard a boy's voice shout: 'There's Oji!'

Ichiro came running towards me, his arms outstretched as though to anticipate an embrace. But then as he reached me, he appeared to check himself, and fixing a solemn expression on his face, held out his hand to be shaken.

'Good day,' he said, in a businesslike manner.

'Well, Ichiro, you're indeed growing into a man. How old are you now?'

'I believe I'm eight. Please come this way, Oji. I have a few things to discuss with you.'

His mother and I followed him to the bench where Noriko was waiting. My younger daughter was wearing a bright dress I had never seen before.

'You're looking very cheerful, Noriko,' I said to her. 'It seems when a daughter leaves home, she immediately begins to get unrecognizable.'

'There's no need for a woman to dress drably simply because she marries,' Noriko said quickly, but she seemed pleased by my compliment none the less.

As I recall, we all sat down for a while beneath the Emperor Taisho and conversed for a while. The reason for our meeting in the park was that my two daughters had wished to spend some time together shopping for fabrics, and I had thus agreed to take Ichiro to lunch at a department store, then spend the afternoon showing him the city centre. Ichiro was impatient to leave, and continued to nudge my arm as we sat talking, saying:

'Oji, let the women chatter between themselves. We have things to attend to.'

My grandson and I found ourselves at the department store slightly after the usual time for lunch, and the restaurant floor was no longer crowded. Ichiro took his time choosing between the various dishes displayed in the cabinets, at one point, turning to me and saying:

'Oji, you guess what my favourite food is now.'

'Hmm. I don't know, Ichiro. Hot-cake? Ice-cream?'

'Spinach! Spinach gives you strength!' He puffed out his chest and flexed his biceps.

'I see. Well now, the Junior Lunch here has some spinach.'

'Junior Lunch is for small children.'

'That may be so, but it's very nice. Oji may order one for himself.'

'All right. I'll have Junior Lunch too. To keep Oji company. But tell the man to give me lots of spinach.'

'Very well, Ichiro.'

'Oji, you're to eat spinach as often as possible. It gives you strength.'

Ichiro chose for us one of the tables beside the row of wide windows, and while waiting for our lunch, continued to place his face against the glass to observe the busy main street four storeys below. I had not seen Ichiro since Setsuko's visit to my home over a year ago – he had not been present at Noriko's wedding on account of a virus – and I was struck by how much he had grown in that time. Not only was he significantly taller, his whole manner had become calmer and less childlike. His eyes in particular seemed to have a much older gaze.

In fact, as I watched Ichiro that day, pressing his face against the glass to see the street below, I could see how much he was coming to resemble his father. There were traces of Setsuko too, but these were to be found mainly in his mannerisms and little facial habits. And of course, I was struck yet again by the similarity Ichiro bore to how my own son, Kenji, had been at that age. I confess I take a strange comfort from observing children inherit these resemblances from other members of the family, and it is my hope that my grandson will retain them into his adult years.

Of course, it is not only when we are children that we are open to these small inheritances; a teacher or mentor whom one admires greatly in early adulthood will leave his mark, and indeed, long after one has come to re-evaluate, perhaps even reject, the bulk of that man's teachings, certain traits will tend to survive, like some shadow of that influence, to remain with one throughout one's life. I am aware, for instance, that certain of my mannerisms – the way I poise my hand when I am explaining something, certain inflexions in my voice when I am trying to convey irony or impatience, even whole phrases I am fond of using that people have come to think of as my own – I am aware these are all traits I originally acquired from Mori-san, my former teacher. And perhaps I will not be flattering myself unduly were I to suppose many of my own pupils will in turn have gained such small inheritances from me. I would hope, furthermore, that in spite of any reassessments they may have come to make concerning those years under my supervision, most of them will have remained grateful for much of what they learnt. Certainly, for my own part, whatever the obvious shortcomings of my former teacher, Seiji Moriyama, or 'Mori-san' as we always called him, whatever occurred between us in the end, I would always acknowledge that those seven years I spent living at his family villa out in the hilly countryside of the Wakaba prefecture were some of the most crucial to my career.

When I try today to summon a picture of Mori-san's villa, I tend to recall one particularly satisfying view of it from up on the mountain path leading to the nearest village. As one climbed that path, the villa would appear down in the hollow below, a dark wooden rectangle set amidst the tall cedar trees. The three long sections of the villa linked to form three sides of the rectangle around a central yard; the fourth side was completed by a cedar fence and gateway, so that the yard was entirely enclosed, and one could imagine how in olden times, it would have been no easy task for hostile visitors to gain entry once that heavy gate had swung shut.

A modern intruder, however, would have found little such difficulty. For though one would have been unable to see this from up on that path, Mori-san's villa was in a state of considerable dilapidation. From up on that path, one would not have guessed how the interiors of the building comprised room after room of torn papering, of tatami floors so worn that in several places there was a danger of falling right through if one trod carelessly. In fact, when I try to recall a picture of the villa seen at closer quarters, what comes to me is an impression of broken roof tiles, decaying latticework, chipped and rotting verandas. Those roofs were forever developing new leaks and after a night of rain, the smell of damp wood and mouldering leaves would pervade every room. And there were those months when insects and moths would invade in such numbers, clinging everywhere to the woodwork, burrowing into every crevice, so that one feared they would cause the place to collapse once and for all.

Of all those rooms, only two or three were in a condition to suggest the splendour the villa must once have possessed. One such room, which filled with a clear light through much of the day, was reserved for special occasions, and I remember how from time to time Mori-san would summon all his pupils – there were ten of us – into that room whenever he had completed a new painting. I recall how before we stepped inside, each of us would pause at the threshold and gasp in admiration at the picture mounted at the centre of the floor. Mori-san, meanwhile, would be attending to a plant perhaps, or looking out of the window, seemingly oblivious to our arrival. Before long, we would all be seated on the floor around the painting, pointing things out to each other in hushed tones: 'And look at the way Sensei has filled in that corner there. Remarkable!' But no one would actually say: 'Sensei, what a marvellous painting,' for it was somehow the convention of these occasions that we behave as though our teacher were not present.

Often a new painting would feature some striking innovation, and a debate of some passion would develop among us. Once, for example, I remember we came into the room to be confronted by a picture of a kneeling woman seen from a peculiarly low point of view – so low that we appeared to be looking up at her from floor level.

'Clearly,' I remember someone asserting, 'the low perspective lends the woman a dignity she would otherwise not have. It is a most astonishing achievement. For in all other respects, she looks a self-pitying sort. It is this tension that gives the painting its subtle power.'

'This may be so,' someone else said. 'The woman may well have a sort of dignity, but that hardly derives from the low viewpoint. It seems clear that Sensei is telling us something much more pertinent. He is saying that the perspective appears low only because we have become so attuned to a particular eye level. It is clearly Sensei's desire to liberate us from such arbitrary and confining habits. He's saying to us, "there's no need to always see things from the usual tired angles". This is why this painting is so inspiring.'

Soon we were all shouting and contradicting each other with our theories about Mori-san's intentions. And although as we argued, we continually stole glances towards our teacher, he gave no indication as to which of our theories he approved of. I recall him simply standing there at the far end of the room, his arms folded, gazing out across the yard through the wood-lattice bars of the window, an amused look on his face. Then, after he had listened to us argue for some time, he turned and said: 'Perhaps you'd all leave me now. There are certain matters I wish to attend to.' At which we all filed out of the room, once more muttering our admiration for the new painting.

As I recount this I am aware that Mori-san's behaviour may strike you as somewhat arrogant. But it is perhaps easier to understand the aloofness he displayed on such occasions if one has oneself been in a position in which one is constantly looked up to and admired. For it is by no means desirable that one be always instructing and pronouncing to one's pupils; there are many situations when it is preferable to remain silent so as to allow them the chance to debate and ponder. As I say, anyone who has been in a position of large influence will appreciate this.

The effect was, in any case, that arguments about our teacher's work could go on for weeks on end. In the continued absence of any explication from Mori-san himself, the tendency was for us to look to one of our number, an artist called Sasaki, who at that point enjoyed the status of being Mori-san's leading pupil. Although as I have said, some arguments could go on a long time, once Sasaki finally made up his mind on a matter, that would usually mark the end of the dispute. Similarly, if Sasaki were to suggest a person's painting was in any way 'disloyal' to our teacher, this would almost always lead to immediate capitulation on the part of the offender – who would then abandon the painting, or in some cases, burn it along with the refuse.

In fact, as I recall, the Tortoise, for several months after our arrival together at the villa, was repeatedly destroying his work under such circumstances. For while I was able to settle easily enough into the way of things there, my companion would again and again produce work displaying elements clearly contrary to our teacher's principles, and I remember many times pleading to my new colleagues on his behalf, explaining that he was not intentionally being disloyal to Mori-san. Often during those early days, the Tortoise would approach me with a distressed air and lead me off to see some half-completed work of his, saying in a low voice: 'Ono-san, please tell me, is this as our teacher would do it?'

And at times, even I became exasperated to discover he had unwittingly employed yet some other obviously offensive element. For it was not as though Mori-san's priorities were at all hard to grasp. The label, 'the modern Utamaro', was often applied to our teacher in those days, and although this was a title conferred all too readily then on any competent artist who specialized in portraying pleasure district women, it tends to sum up Mori-san's concerns rather well. For Mori-san was consciously trying to 'modernize' the Utamaro tradition; in many of his most notable paintings – 'Tying a Dance Drum', say, or 'After a Bath' – the woman is seen from the back in classic Utamaro fashion. Various other such classic features recur in his work: the woman holding a towel to her face, the woman combing out her long hair. And Mori-san made extensive use of the traditional device of expressing emotion through the textiles which the woman holds or wears rather than through the look on her face. But at the same time, his work was full of European influences, which the more staunch admirers of Utamaro would have regarded as iconoclastic; he had, for instance, long abandoned the use of the traditional dark outline to define his shapes, preferring instead the Western use of blocks of colour, with light and shade to create a three-dimensional appearance. And no doubt, he had taken his cue from the Europeans in what was his most central concern: the use of subdued colours. Mori-san's wish was to evoke a certain melancholy, nocturnal atmosphere around his women, and throughout the years I studied under him, he experimented extensively with colours in an attempt to capture the feel of lantern light. Because of this, it was something of a hallmark of Mori-san's work that a lantern would always figure somewhere in the picture, by implication if not in actuality. It was perhaps typical of the Tortoise's slowness in grasping the essentials of Mori-san's art that even after a year at the villa, he was using colours that created quite the wrong effect, then wondering why he was again being accused of disloyalty when he had remembered to include a lantern in his composition.

For all my pleadings, the likes of Sasaki had little patience for the Tortoise's difficulties and at times the atmosphere threatened to become as hostile for my companion as any he had experienced at Master Takeda's firm. And then – I believe it was some time during our second year at the villa – a change came over Sasaki, a change that was to lead to his suffering hostility of an altogether harsher and darker nature than anything he had ever orchestrated against the Tortoise.

One supposes all groups of pupils tend to have a leader figure – someone whose abilities the teacher has singled out as an example for the others to follow. And it is this leading pupil, by virtue of his having the strongest grasp of his teacher's ideas, who will tend to function, as did Sasaki, as the main interpreter of those ideas to the less able or less experienced pupils. But by the same token, it is this same leading pupil who is most likely to see shortcomings in the teacher's work, or else develop views of his own divergent from those of his teacher. In theory, of course, a good teacher should accept this tendency – indeed, welcome it as a sign that he has brought his pupil to a point of maturity. In practice, however, the emotions involved can be quite complicated. Sometimes, when one has nurtured a gifted pupil long and hard, it is difficult to see any such maturing of talent as anything other than treachery, and some regrettable situations are apt to arise.

Certainly, what we did to Sasaki following his dispute with our teacher was quite unwarranted, and there seems little to be gained in my recalling such things here. I do, however, have some vivid recollections of that night when Sasaki finally left us.

Most of us had already turned in. I was myself lying awake in the darkness in one of those dilapidated rooms, when I heard Sasaki's voice calling to someone a little way down the veranda. He seemed to receive no answer from whoever it was he was addressing, and eventually there came the sounds of a screen sliding shut and Sasaki's footsteps coming nearer. I heard him stop at another room and say something, but again he seemed to be met only with silence. His footsteps came still closer, then I heard him slide open the screen of the room next to mine.

'You and I have been good friends for many years,' I heard him say. 'Won't you at least speak to me?'

There was no response from the person he had addressed. Then Sasaki said:

'Won't you just tell me where the paintings are?'

There was still no response. But as I lay there in the

142

darkness, I could hear the sound of rats scuttling under the floorboards of that neighbouring room, and it seemed to me this noise was some sort of reply.

'If you find them so offensive,' Sasaki's voice continued, 'there's no sense in your keeping them. But they happen to mean a great deal to me at this moment. I wish to take them with me, wherever it is I'm going. I've nothing else to take with me.'

Again, there came the scuttling noise of rats in reply, then a long silence. Indeed, the silence went on for so long, I thought perhaps Sasaki had walked off into the darkness and I had failed to hear him. But then I heard him say again:

'These past few days, the others have done some terrible things to me. But what has hurt me the most has been your refusal to give me even one word of comfort.'

There was another silence. Then Sasaki said: 'Won't you even look at me now and wish me well?'

Eventually, I heard the screen slide shut, and the sounds of Sasaki stepping down from the veranda and walking away across the yard.

After his departure, Sasaki was hardly mentioned at the villa and on the few occasions he was, he tended to be referred to simply as 'the traitor'. Indeed, I am reminded of just how much Sasaki's memory was prone to cause offence amongst us when I recall what occurred once or twice during those slanging contests we often indulged in.

On warmer days, because we tended to leave the screens of our rooms wide open, several of us congregating in a room might catch sight of another group similarly gathered on the opposite wing. This situation would soon lead to someone calling out across the yard a witty provocation, and before long, both groups would be assembled out on their respective verandas, shouting insults across at each other. This behaviour may sound absurd when I recount it, but there was something about the architecture of the villa and the echoing acoustics it produced when one shouted from one wing to another, that somehow encouraged us to indulge in these childish contests. The insults could be far-ranging – making fun of someone's manly prowess, say, or of a painting someone had just completed – but for the most part were devoid of any intent to wound, and I recall many highly amusing exchanges which had both sides red with laughter. Indeed, by and large, my memories of these exchanges sum up well enough the competitive yet family-like intimacy we enjoyed during those years at the villa. And yet, when once or twice Sasaki's name was invoked during the course of these insults, things suddenly got out of hand, with colleagues abandoning boundaries and actually scrapping in the yard. It did not take us long to learn that to compare someone to 'the traitor', even in fun, was never likely to be received in good humour.

You may gather from such recollections that our devotion to our teacher and to his principles was fierce and total. And it is easy with hindsight – once the shortcomings of an influence have become obvious – to be critical of a teacher who fosters such a climate. But then again, anyone who has held ambitions on a grand scale, anyone who has been in a position to achieve something large and has felt the need to impart his ideas as thoroughly as possible, will have some sympathy for the way Mori-san conducted things. For though it may seem a little foolish now in the light of what became of his career, it was Mori-san's wish at that time to do nothing less than change fundamentally the identity of painting as practised in our city. It was with no less a goal in mind that he devoted so much of his time and wealth to the nurturing of pupils, and it is perhaps important to remember this when making judgements concerning my former teacher.

His influence over us was not, of course, confined merely to the realms of painting. We lived throughout those years almost entirely in accordance with his values and lifestyle, and this entailed spending much time exploring the city's 'floating world' – the night-time world of pleasure, entertainment and drink which formed the backdrop for all our paintings. I always feel a certain nostalgia now in recalling the city centre as it was in those days; the streets were not so filled with the noise of traffic, and the factories had yet to take the fragrance of seasonal blossoms from the night air. A favourite haunt of ours was a small teahouse beside the canal in Kojima Street called 'Water Lanterns' – for indeed, the lanterns of the establishment could be seen reflected in the canal as one approached. The proprietress was an old friend of Mori-san's, which ensured we always received generous treatment, and I recall some memorable nights there, singing and drinking with our hostesses. Our other regular haunt was an archery parlour in Nagata Street, where the proprietress never tired of reminding us how years before, when she had been working as a geisha in Akihara, Mori-san had used her as a model for a series of wood-block prints which had proved immensely popular. Some six or seven young women hosted that archery parlour and after a while we each had our own favourites with whom to exchange pipes and pass away the night.

Neither was our merrymaking limited to these expeditions into the city. Mori-san seemed to have a never-ending line of acquaintances from the world of entertaining, and impoverished troupes of wandering actors, dancers and musicians were forever arriving at the villa to be greeted as long-lost friends. Large quantities of liquor would then be produced, our visitors would sing and dance through the night, and before long someone would have to be sent out to awaken the wine seller at the nearest village for replenishments. One regular visitor of those days was a story-teller called Maki, a fat jolly man who could reduce us all to helpless laughter one moment and tears of sadness the next with his renderings of the old tales. Years later, I came across Maki a few times at the Migi-Hidari, and we would reminisce with some amazement about those nights at the villa. Maki was convinced he remembered many of those parties continuing straight through one night, through the following day and into a second night. Although I could not be so certain of this, I had to admit to recollections of Mori-san's villa in the daytime, littered everywhere with sleeping or exhausted bodies, some of them collapsed out in the yard with the sun beating down on them.

I have, however, a more vivid memory concerning one such night. I can recall walking alone across the central yard, grateful for the fresh night air, having for a moment escaped the revellings. I remember I walked over to the entrance of the storeroom, and before going in, glanced back across the yard towards the room where my companions and our visitors were entertaining each other. I could see numerous silhouettes dancing behind the paper screens, and a singer's voice came drifting out through the night to me.

I had made my way to the storeroom because it was one of the few places in the villa where there was a chance of remaining undisturbed for any length of time. I imagine in days gone by, when the villa had housed guards and retainers, the room had been used for storing weapons and armour. But when I stepped inside that night and lit the lantern hanging above the door, I found the floor so cluttered with every sort of object it was impossible to cross it without hopping from space to space; everywhere were stacks of old canvasses tied together with rope, broken easels, all manner of pots and jars with brushes or sticks protruding. I negotiated my way to a clearing on the floor and sat down. The lantern above the door, I noticed, was causing the objects around me to throw exaggerated shadows; it was an eerie effect, as though I were sitting in some grotesque miniature cemetery.

I suppose I must have become quite lost in my broodings, for I recall being startled by the sound of the storeroom door sliding open. I looked up to see Mori-san in the doorway and said hurriedly: 'Good evening, Sensei.'

Possibly the lantern above the door did not give sufficient

light to illuminate my part of the room, or perhaps it was simply that my face was in shadow. In any case, Mori-san peered forward and asked:

'Who is that? Ono?'

'Indeed, Sensei.'

He continued to peer forward for a moment. Then, taking the lantern down from the beam and holding it out before him, he began to make his way towards me, stepping carefully through the objects on the floor. As he did so, the lantern in his hand caused shadows to move all around us. I hastened to clear a space for him, but before I could do so, Mori-san had seated himself a little way away on an old wooden chest. He gave a sigh and said:

'I stepped out for a little fresh air, and I saw this light on in here. Darkness everywhere, except this one light. And I thought to myself, now that storeroom's hardly a place for lovers to be hiding away. Whoever's in there must be in a lonely mood.'

'I suppose I must have been sitting here in a dream, Sensei. I had no intention of remaining here so long.'

He had placed the lantern on the floor beside him, so that from where I sat, I could see only his silhouette. 'One of those dancing girls appeared very taken with you earlier,' he said. 'She'll be disappointed to find you've vanished now the night's here.'

'I didn't mean to appear rude to our guests, Sensei. Like yourself, I simply came out for some fresh air.'

We were silent for a moment. Across the yard, our companions could be heard singing and clapping their hands in time.

'Well, Ono,' Mori-san said eventually, 'what do you make of my old friend Gisaburo? Quite a character.'

'Indeed, Sensei. He seems a most affable gentleman.'

'He may be dressed in rags these days, but he was once quite a celebrity. And as he showed us tonight, he still has much of his old skill left.'

'Indeed.'

'So then, Ono. What is it that worries you?'

'Worries me, Sensei? Why, nothing at all.'

'Can it be that you find something a little offensive about old Gisaburo?'

'Not at all, Sensei.' I laughed self-consciously. 'Why, not at all. A most charming gentleman.'

For a little time after that, we talked of other matters, of anything which came to mind. But when Mori-san had turned the conversation back once more to my 'worries', when it became clear he was prepared to sit there waiting until I unburdened myself, I finally said:

'Gisaburo-san does indeed appear to be the most good-hearted gentleman. He and his dancers have been most kind to entertain us. But then I cannot help thinking, Sensei, we have been visited by their like so often these past few months.'

Mori-san gave no reply, so I continued:

'Forgive me, Sensei, I mean no disrespect to Gisaburo-san and his friends. But at times I am a little puzzled. I am puzzled that we artists should be devoting so much of our time enjoying the company of those like Gisaburo-san.'

I believe it was around this point that my teacher rose to his feet and, lantern in hand, made his way across the floor towards the back wall of the storeroom. The wall had previously been in darkness, but as he held the lantern up to it, three wood-block prints, hung one below the other, became sharply illuminated. Each of these portrayed a geisha adjusting her coiffure, each seated on the floor and viewed from the back. Mori-san studied the pictures for a few moments, moving the lantern from one to the next. Then he shook his head and muttered to himself: 'Fatally flawed. Fatally flawed by trivial concerns.' A few seconds later, he added without turning from the pictures: 'But one always feels affection for one's early works. Perhaps you'll feel the same one day for the work you've done here.' Then he shook his head again, saying: 'But these are all fatally flawed, Ono.'

'I cannot agree, Sensei,' I said. 'I think those prints are marvellous examples of how an artist's talent can transcend the limitations of a particular style. I've often thought it a great shame Sensei's early prints should be confined to such rooms as these. Surely they should be open to display along with his paintings.'

Mori-san remained absorbed by his pictures. 'Fatally flawed,' he repeated. 'But I suppose I was very young.' He moved his lantern again, causing one picture to fade into shadow and another to appear. Then he said: 'These are all scenes from a certain geisha house in Honcho. A very well-regarded one in my younger days. Gisaburo and I often used to visit such places together.' Then after a moment or two, he said again: 'These are fatally flawed, Ono.'

'But Sensei, I cannot see what faults even the most discerning eye would see in these prints.'

He continued to study the pictures for a few moments more, then began to come back across the room. It seemed to me that he took an inordinate amount of time negotiating his way through the objects on the floor; at times, I would hear him mumbling to himself and the sound of his feet pushing away a jar or box. Indeed, I once or twice thought Mori-san was actually searching for something – perhaps more of his early prints – amidst the chaotic piles, but eventually he seated himself back on the old wooden chest and drew a sigh. After a few further moments of silence, he said:

'Gisaburo is an unhappy man. He's had a sad life. His talent has gone to ruin. Those he once loved have long since died or deserted him. Even in our younger days, he was already a lonely, sad character.' Mori-san paused a moment. Then he went on: 'But then sometimes we used to drink and enjoy ourselves with the women of the pleasure quarters, and Gisaburo would become happy. Those women would tell him all the things he wanted to hear, and for the night anyway, he'd be able to believe them. Once the morning came, of course, he was too intelligent a man to go on believing such things. But Gisaburo didn't value those nights any the less for that. The best things, he always used to say, are put together of a night and vanish with the morning. What people call the floating world, Ono, was a world Gisaburo knew how to value.'

Mori-san paused again. As before, I could see his form only in silhouette, but it was my impression he was listening to the sounds of the merrymaking from across the yard. Then he said: 'He's older and sadder now, but he's changed little in many respects. Tonight he's happy, just as he used to be in those pleasure houses.' He drew a long breath, as though he were smoking tobacco. Then he went on: 'The finest, most fragile beauty an artist can hope to capture drifts within those pleasure houses after dark. And on nights like these, Ono, some of that beauty drifts into our own quarters here. But as for those pictures up there, they don't even hint at these transitory, illusory qualities. They're deeply flawed, Ono.'

'But Sensei, to my eyes, those prints suggest most impressively these very things.'

'I was very young when I prepared those prints. I suspect the reason I couldn't celebrate the floating world was that I couldn't bring myself to believe in its worth. Young men are often guilt-ridden about pleasure, and I suppose I was no different. I suppose I thought that to pass away one's time in such places, to spend one's skills celebrating things so intangible and transient, I suppose I thought it all rather wasteful, all rather decadent. It's hard to appreciate the beauty of a world when one doubts its very validity.'

I thought about this, then said: 'Indeed, Sensei, I admit what you say may well apply in respect to my own work. I will do all I can to put matters right.'

Mori-san appeared not to hear me. 'But I've long since lost all such doubts, Ono,' he continued. 'When I am an old man, when I look back over my life and see I have devoted it to the task of capturing the unique beauty of that world, I believe I will be well satisfied. And no man will make me believe I've wasted my time.'

It is possible, of course, that Mori-san did not use those exact words. Indeed, on reflection, such phrases sound rather more like the sort of thing I myself would declare to my own pupils after we had been drinking a little at the Migi-Hidari. 'As the new generation of Japanese artists, you have a great responsibility towards the culture of this nation. I am proud to have the likes of you as my pupils. And while I may deserve only the smallest praise for my own paintings, when I come to look back over my life and remember I have nurtured and assisted·the careers of all of you here, why then no man will make me believe I have wasted my time.' And whenever I made some such statement, all those young men congregated around the table would drown each other out in protest at the way I had dismissed my own paintings – which, they clamoured to inform me, were without doubt great works assured of their place in posterity. But then again, as I have said, many phrases and expressions which came to be most characteristic of me I actually inherited from Mori-san, and so it is quite possible that those were my teacher's exact words that night, instilled in me by the powerful impression they made on me at the time.

But again I have drifted. I was trying to recall the lunch I had at the department store with my grandson last month following that annoying conversation with Setsuko in Kawabe Park. In fact, I believe I was remembering in particular Ichiro's extolling of spinach.

Once our lunch had arrived, I recall, Ichiro sat there preoccupied with the spinach on his plate, sometimes prodding at it with his spoon. Then he looked up and said: 'Oji, you watch!'

My grandson proceeded to pile as much spinach as possible on to the spoon, then raised it high into the air and began pouring it into his mouth. His method resembled someone drinking the last dregs from a bottle.

'Ichiro,' I said, 'I'm not sure that's such good manners.'

But my grandson continued putting more spinach into his mouth, all the time chewing vigorously. He put down his spoon only when it was empty and his cheeks were full to bursting. Then, still chewing, he fixed a stern expression on his face, thrust out his chest and began punching at the air around him.

'What are you doing, Ichiro? You tell me now what you're up to.'

'You guess, Oji!' he said, through the spinach.

'Hmm. I don't know, Ichiro. A man drinking sake and fighting. No? Then you tell me. Oji can't guess.'

'Popeye Sailorman!'

'What's that, Ichiro? Another of your heroes?'

'Popeye Sailorman eats spinach. Spinach makes him strong.' He thrust out his chest again and threw more punches at the air.

'I see, Ichiro,' I said, laughing. 'Spinach is a wonderful food indeed.'

'Does sake make you strong?'

I smiled and shook my head. 'Sake can make you believe you're strong. But in reality, Ichiro, you're no stronger than before you drank it.'

'Why do men drink sake then, Oji?'

'I don't know, Ichiro. Perhaps because for a little while, they can believe they're stronger. But sake doesn't really make a man stronger.'

'Spinach makes you really strong.'

'Then spinach is much better than sake. You go on eating spinach, Ichiro. But look, what about all these other things on your plate?'

'I like drinking sake too. And whisky. At home, there's a bar I always go to.'

'Is that so, Ichiro. I think it's better you go on eating spinach. As you say, that makes you really strong.'

'I like sake best. I drink ten bottles every night. Then I drink ten bottles of whisky.'

'Is that so, Ichiro. Now that's real drinking indeed. This must be a real headache for Mother.'

'Women never understand about us men drinking,' Ichiro said, and turned his attention to the lunch in front of him. But soon he looked up again and said: 'Oji's coming for supper tonight.'

'That's right, Ichiro. I expect Aunt Noriko will prepare something very nice.'

'Aunt Noriko's bought some sake. She said Oji and Uncle Taro will drink it all up.'

'Well, we may do indeed. I'm sure the women will like a little too. But she's right, Ichiro. Sake's mainly for the men.'

'Oji, what happens if women drink sake?'

'Hmm. There's no telling. Women aren't as strong as we men are, Ichiro. So perhaps they'll get drunk very quickly.'

'Aunt Noriko might get drunk! She might have a tiny cupful and get completely drunk!'

I gave a laugh. 'Yes, that's quite possible.'

'Aunt Noriko might get completely drunk! She'll sing songs then fall asleep at the table!'

'Well, Ichiro,' I said, still laughing, 'we men had better keep the sake to ourselves then, hadn't we?'

'Men are stronger, so we can drink more.'

'That's right, Ichiro. We'd best keep the sake to ourselves.'

Then, after I had thought for a moment, I added: 'I suppose you're eight years old now, Ichiro. You're growing to be a big man. Who knows? Perhaps Oji will see to it you get some sake tonight.'

My grandson looked at me with a slightly threatened expression, and said nothing. I smiled at him, then glanced out at the pale grey sky through the large windows beside us.

'You never met your Uncle Kenji, Ichiro. When he was your age, he was as big and strong as you are now. I remember he had his first taste of sake at around your age. I'll see to it, Ichiro, you get a small taste tonight.'

Ichiro seemed to consider this for a moment. Then he said:

'Mother might be trouble.'

'Don't worry about your mother, Ichiro. Your Oji will be able to handle her.'

Ichiro shook his head wearily. 'Women never understand men drinking,' he remarked.

'Well, it's time a man like you tasted a little sake. Don't you worry, Ichiro, you leave your mother to Oji. We can't have the women bossing us around now, can we?'

My grandson remained absorbed in his thoughts for a moment. Then suddenly he said very loudly:

'Aunt Noriko might get drunk!'

I laughed. 'We'll see, Ichiro,' I said.

'Aunt Noriko might get completely drunk!'

It was perhaps fifteen minutes or so later, as we were waiting for ice-cream, that Ichiro asked in a thoughtful voice.

'Oji, did you know Yujiro Naguchi?'

'You must mean Yukio Naguchi, Ichiro. No, I never knew him personally.'

My grandson did not respond, apparently absorbed by his reflection in the glass pane beside him.

'Your mother,' I went on, 'also seemed to have Mr Naguchi on her mind when I was speaking with her in the park this morning. I take it the adults were discussing him at supper last night, were they?'

For a moment, Ichiro went on gazing at his reflection. Then he turned to me and asked:

'Was Mr Naguchi like Oji?'

'Was Mr Naguchi like me? Well, your mother for one doesn't seem to think so. It was just something I said to your Uncle Taro once, Ichiro, it was nothing very serious. Your mother seems to have picked it up far too earnestly. I hardly remember what I was talking to Uncle Taro about at the time, but Oji just happened to suggest he had one or two things in common with people like Mr Naguchi. Now you tell me, Ichiro, what were the adults all saying last night?'

'Oji, why did Mr Naguchi kill himself?'

'That's hard to say for sure, Ichiro. I never knew Mr Naguchi personally.'

'But was he a bad man?'

'No. He wasn't a bad man. He was just someone who worked very hard doing what he thought was for the best. But you see, Ichiro, when the war ended, things were very different. The songs Mr Naguchi composed had become very famous, not just in this city, but all over Japan. They were sung on the radio and in bars. And the likes of your Uncle Kenji sang them when they were marching or before a battle. And after the war, Mr Naguchi thought his songs had been – well – a sort of mistake. He thought of all the people who had been killed, all the little boys your age, Ichiro, who no longer had parents, he thought of all these things and he thought perhaps his songs were a mistake. And he felt he should apologize. To everyone who was left. To little boys who no longer had parents. And to parents who had lost little boys like you. To all these people, he wanted to say sorry. I think that's why he killed himself. Mr Naguchi wasn't a bad man at all, Ichiro. He was brave to admit the mistakes he'd made. He was very brave and honourable.'

Ichiro was watching me with a thoughtful expression. I gave a laugh and said: 'What's the matter, Ichiro?'

My grandson seemed about to speak, but then turned again to look at his face reflected in the glass.

'Your Oji never meant anything by saying he was like Mr Naguchi,' I said. 'It was a sort of joke he was making, that's all. You tell your mother that, the next time you hear her talking about Mr Naguchi. Because from what she was saying this morning, she's picked the whole thing up quite wrongly. What's the matter, Ichiro? Suddenly so quiet.'

After lunch we spent some time wandering around shops in the city centre, looking at toys and books. Then, towards the latter part of the afternoon, I treated Ichiro to another ice-cream at one of those smart refectories along Sakurabashi Street, before making our way to Taro and Noriko's new apartment in Izumimachi.

The Izumimachi area, as you may be aware, has now become very popular with young couples from the better backgrounds, and there is certainly a clean, respectable atmosphere there. But most of the newly-built apartment blocks that have drawn these young couples seem to me unimaginative and constrictive. Taro and Noriko's apartment, for instance, is a small two-room affair on the third floor: the ceilings are low, sounds come in from neighbouring apartments and the view from the window is principally of the opposite block and its windows. I am sure it is not simply because I am accustomed to my more spacious, traditional house that even after a short time I begin to find the place claustrophobic. Noriko, however, seems very proud of her apartment, and is forever extolling its 'modern' qualities. It is, apparently, very easy to keep clean, and the ventilation most effective; in particular, the kitchens and bathrooms throughout the block are of Western design and are, so my daughter assures me, infinitely more practical than, say, the arrangements in my own house.

However convenient the kitchen, it is very small, and when I stepped inside it that evening to see how my daughters were progressing with the meal, there seemed no space for me to stand. Because of this, and because my daughters both seemed busy, I did not remain chatting with them long. But I did remark at one point:

'You know, Ichiro was telling me earlier he's keen to taste a little sake.'

Setsuko and Noriko, who had been standing side by side slicing vegetables, both stopped and glanced up at me.

'I gave it some thought and decided we could let him have a small taste,' I went on. 'But perhaps you should dilute it with some water.'

'I'm sorry, Father,' Setsuko said, 'but you're suggesting Ichiro drink sake tonight?'

'Just a little. He's a growing boy after all. But as I say, you'd best dilute it.'

My daughters exchanged glances. Then Noriko said: 'Father, he's only eight years old.'

'There's no harm so long as you mix it with water. You women may not understand, but these things mean a great deal to a young boy like Ichiro. It's a question of pride. He'll remember it for the rest of his life.'

'Father, this is nonsense,' said Noriko. 'Ichiro would just be sick.'

'Nonsense or not, I've thought this over carefully. You women sometimes don't have enough sympathy for a boy's pride.' I pointed to the sake bottle standing on a shelf above their heads. 'Just a small drop will do.'

With that, I began to leave. But then I heard Noriko say: 'Setsuko, it's out of the question. I don't know what Father can be thinking.'

'Why all this fuss?' I said, turning at the doorway. Behind me, from the main room, I could hear Taro and my grandson laughing over something. I lowered my voice and continued:

'Anyway, I've promised him now, he's looking forward to it. You women sometimes just don't understand about pride.'

I was making to leave again, when this time it was Setsuko who spoke.

'It is very kind of Father to consider Ichiro's feelings so carefully. However, I wonder if it wouldn't perhaps be best to wait till Ichiro is a little older.'

I gave a small laugh. 'You know, I remember your mother protesting in just the same way when I decided to let Kenji have a taste of sake at this age. Well, it certainly did your brother no harm.'

I regretted immediately introducing Kenji into such a trivial disagreement. Indeed, I believe I was momentarily quite annoyed with myself, and it is possible I did not pay much attention to what Setsuko said next. In any case, it seems to me she said something like:

'There is no doubt Father devoted the most careful thought to my brother's upbringing. Nevertheless, in the light of what came to pass, we can perhaps see that on one or two points at least, Mother may in fact have had the more correct ideas.'

To be fair, it is possible she did not say anything quite so unpleasant. Indeed, it is possible I misinterpreted entirely what she actually said, for I distinctly recall Noriko not reacting at all to her sister's words other than to turn wearily back to her vegetables. Besides, I would not have thought Setsuko capable of introducing so gratuitously such a note to the conversation. Then again, when I consider the sort of insinuations Setsuko had been making in Kawabe Park earlier that same day, I suppose I have to admit the possibility that she did say something along such lines. In any case, I recall Setsuko concluding by saying:

'Besides, I fear Suichi would not wish Ichiro to drink sake until he is a little older. But it is most kind of Father to have given such consideration to Ichiro's feelings.'

Conscious that Ichiro might overhear our conversation, and not wishing to put a cloud over what was a rare family reunion, I let the argument rest there and left the kitchen. For a while after that, as I recall, I sat in the main room with Taro and Ichiro, exchanging enjoyable talk as we awaited supper.

We eventually sat down to eat an hour or so later. As we were doing so, Ichiro reached over to the sake flask on the table, tapped it with his fingers and looked over at me knowingly. I smiled at him, but said nothing.

The women had prepared a splendid meal and the conversation was soon flowing effortlessly. At one point, Taro had us all laughing with the story of a colleague of his at work, who through a mixture of misfortune and his own comical stupidity, had gained a reputation for never meeting deadlines. Once, while relating this story, Taro said:

'Indeed, things have got to such a state it seems our superiors have taken to calling him "the Tortoise". During a meeting recently, Mr Hayasaka forgot himself and actually announced: "We'll hear the Tortoise's report, then break for lunch." '

'Is that so?' I exclaimed with some surprise. 'That's very curious. I myself once had a colleague who had that nickname. For much the same reasons, it would seem.'

But Taro did not seem particularly struck by this coincidence. He nodded politely, and said: 'I remember at school, too, there was a pupil we all called "the Tortoise". In fact, just as every group has a natural leader, I suspect every group has its "Tortoise".'

With that, Taro returned to the relating of his anecdote. Of course, now I come to think of it, I suppose my son-in-law was quite correct; most groups of peers would have their 'Tortoise', even if the name itself is not always used. Amongst my own pupils, for instance, it was Shintaro who fulfilled such a role. This is not to deny Shintaro's basic competence; but when placed alongside the likes of Kuroda, it was as though his talent lacked an entire dimension.

I suppose I do not on the whole greatly admire the Tortoises of this world. While one may appreciate their plodding steadiness and ability to survive, one suspects their lack of frankness, their capacity for treachery. And I suppose, in the end, one despises their unwillingness to take chances in the name of ambition or for the sake of a principle they claim to believe in. Their like will never fall victim to the sort of grand catastrophe that, say, Akira Sugimura suffered over Kawabe Park; but by the same token, notwithstanding the small sorts of respectability they may sometimes achieve as schoolteachers or whatever, they will never accomplish anything above the mediocre.

It is true, I grew quite fond of the Tortoise during those years we spent together at Mori-san's villa, but then I do not believe I ever respected him as an equal. This had to do with the very nature of our friendship, which had been forged during the days of the Tortoise's persecution at Master Takeda's firm and then through his difficulties in our early months at the villa; somehow, after a time, it had cemented itself into one in which he was perpetually indebted to me for some undefined 'support' I gave him. Long after he had grasped how to paint without arousing the hostility of the others at the villa, long after he had come to be generally well liked for his pleasant, obliging nature, he was still saying to me things like:

'I'm so grateful to you, Ono-san. It's due to you I'm treated so well here.'

In one sense, of course, the Tortoise *was* indebted to me; for clearly, without my initiative, he would never have considered leaving Master Takeda's to become Mori-san's pupil. He had been extremely reluctant to take such an adventurous step, but once having been compelled to do so, he had never doubted the decision. Indeed, the Tortoise held Mori-san in such reverence that for a long time – for the first two years at least – I cannot recall his being able to hold a conversation with our teacher, other than to mumble: 'Yes, Sensei' or 'No, Sensei.'

Throughout those years, the Tortoise continued to paint as slowly as he ever did, but it did not occur to anyone to hold this against him. In fact, there were a number of others who worked just as slowly, and this faction actually had a tendency to mock those of us with faster working habits. I remember they labelled us 'the engineers', comparing the intense and frantic way we worked once an idea had struck with an engine driver shovelling on coal for fear the steam would at any moment run out. We in turn named the slow faction 'the backwarders'. A 'backwarder' was originally a term used at the villa for someone who, in a room crowded with people working at easels, insisted on stepping backwards every few minutes to view his canvas – with the result that he continually collided with colleagues working behind him. It was of course quite unfair to suggest that because an artist liked to take time with a painting – stepping back, as it were, metaphorically – he was any more likely to be guilty of this antisocial habit, but then we enjoyed the very provocativeness of the label. Indeed, I recall a lot of good-humoured bantering concerning 'engineers' and 'back-warders'.

In truth, though, just about all of us were prone to be guilty of 'backwarding', and because of this, we would as far as possible avoid crowding together when working. In the summer months, many of my colleagues would set up easels spaced out at points along the verandas, or else out in the yard itself, while others insisted on reserving large numbers of rooms because they liked to circulate from room to room according to the light. The Tortoise and I always tended to work in the disused kitchen – a large, barn-like annex behind one of the wings.

The floor as one entered was of trodden earth, but towards the back was a raised boarded platform, wide enough for our two easels. The low crossbeams with their hooks – from which once hung pots and other kitchen utensils – and the bamboo racks on the walls, proved most useful for our brushes, rags, paints and so on. And I can recall how the Tortoise and I would fill a large old blackened pot full of water, carry it on to the platform and suspend it on the old pulleys so that it hung at shoulder height between us as we painted.

I remember one afternoon, we were painting in the old kitchen as usual, when the Tortoise said to me:

'I'm very curious, Ono-san, about your present painting. It must be something very special.'

I smiled without taking my eyes from my work. 'Why do you say that? It's just a little experiment of mine, that's all.'

'But Ono-san, it's a long time since I've seen you working with such intensity. And you've requested privacy. You haven't requested privacy now for at least two years. Not since you were preparing "Lion-dance" for your first exhibition.'

I should perhaps explain here that occasionally, whenever

an artist felt a particular work would be hampered by comments of any sort before its completion, he would 'request privacy' for that work, and it was then understood that no one would attempt to look at it until such time as the artist withdrew his request. This was a sensible arrangement, living and working as we did so closely, and gave one room to take risks without fear of making a fool of oneself.

'Is it really so noticeable?' I said. 'I thought I was hiding my excitement rather well.'

'You must be forgetting, Ono-san. We've been painting side by side for almost eight years now. Oh yes, I can tell this is something quite special for you.'

'Eight years,' I remarked. 'I suppose that's right.'

'Indeed, Ono-san. And it's been a privilege to work so close to one of your talent. More than a little humbling at times, but a great privilege nonetheless.'

'You exaggerate,' I said, smiling and continuing to paint.

'Not at all, Ono-san. Indeed, I feel I would never have progressed as I have over these years without the constant inspiration of seeing your works appearing before my eyes. No doubt you've noted the extent to which my modest "Autumn Girl" owes itself to your magnificent "Girl at Sunset". One of many attempts on my part, Ono-san, to emulate your brilliance. A feeble attempt, I realize, but then Mori-san was good enough to praise it as a significant step forward for me.'

'I wonder now.' I ceased my brush strokes for a moment and looked at my work. 'I wonder if this painting here will also inspire you.'

I continued to regard my half-finished painting for a moment, then glanced across to my friend over the ancient pot suspended between us. The Tortoise was painting happily, unaware of my gaze. He had put on a little more flesh since the days I had first known him at Master Takeda's, and the harassed, fearful look of those days had been largely replaced by an air of childlike contentment. In fact, I recall someone around that time comparing the Tortoise to a puppy who had just been petted, and indeed, this description was not inappropriate to the impression I received as I watched him paint that afternoon in the old kitchen.

'Tell me, Tortoise,' I said to him. 'You're quite happy with your work at present, are you?'

'Most happy, thank you, Ono-san,' he replied immediately. Then glancing up, he added hastily with a grin: 'Of course, it has a long way to go before it can stand alongside your work, Ono-san.'

His eyes returned to his painting and I watched him working for a few more moments. Then I asked:

'You don't consider sometimes trying some . . . some new approaches?'

'New approaches, Ono-san?' he said, not looking up.

'Tell me, Tortoise, don't you have ambitions to one day produce paintings of genuine importance? I don't mean simply work that we may admire and praise amongst ourselves here at the villa. I refer to work of real importance. Work that will be a significant contribution to the people of our nation. It's to this end, Tortoise, I talk of the need for a new approach.'

I had watched him carefully as I said all this, but the Tortoise did not pause in his painting.

'To tell you the truth, Ono-san,' he said, 'someone in my humble position is always trying new approaches. But over this past year, I believe I'm beginning to find the right path at last. You see, Ono-san, I've noticed Mori-san looking at my work more and more closely this past year. I know he's pleased with me. Who knows, sometime in the future, I may even be permitted to exhibit alongside yourself and Mori-san.' Then at last he looked across to me and laughed self-consciously. 'Forgive me, Ono-san. Just a fantasy to keep me persevering.'

I decided to let the matter drop. I had intended to try again at some later date to draw my friend into my confidence, but as it turned out, I was pre-empted by events.

It was a sunny morning a few days after the conversation I have just recounted, when I stepped into the old kitchen to discover the Tortoise standing up on the platform at the back of that barn-like building, staring towards me. It took my eyes a few seconds to adjust to the shade after the brightness of the morning outside, but I soon noticed the guarded, almost alarmed expression he was wearing; indeed, there was something in the way he raised an arm awkwardly towards his chest before letting it fall again that suggested he expected me to attack him. He had made no attempt to set up his easel or otherwise prepare for the day's work, and when I greeted him he remained silent. I came nearer and asked:

'Is something wrong?'

'Ono-san . . .' he muttered, but said no more. Then as I came up to the platform, he looked nervously to his left. I followed his gaze to my unfinished painting, covered over and stacked faced against the wall. The Tortoise gestured nervously towards it and said:

'Ono-san, is this a joke of yours?'

'No, Tortoise,' I said, climbing up on to the platform. 'It's no joke at all.'

I walked over to the painting, pulled off the drapes and turned it around to face us. The Tortoise immediately averted his eyes.

'My friend,' I said, 'you were once brave enough to listen to me and we took together an important step in our careers. I'd ask you now to consider taking another step forward with me.'

The Tortoise continued to hold his face away. He said:

'Ono-san, is our teacher aware of this painting?'

'No, not yet. But I suppose I may as well show it to him. From now on, I intend to always paint along these lines. Tortoise, look at my painting. Let me explain to you what I'm trying to do. Then perhaps we can again take an important step forward together.'

At last he turned to look at me.

'Ono-san,' he said, in a near whisper, 'you are a traitor. Now please excuse me.'

With that, he hurried out of the building.

The painting which had so upset the Tortoise was one entitled 'Complacency', and although it did not remain in my possession for long, such was my investment in it at that time that its details have stayed imprinted on my memory; indeed, had I the desire to do so, I feel I could quite accurately recreate that painting today. The inspiration behind it had been a small scene I had witnessed some weeks previously, something I had seen while out walking with Matsuda.

We were, I recall, on our way to meet some of Matsuda's colleagues from the Okada-Shingen Society to whom he wished to introduce me. It was towards the end of summer; the hottest days were past, but I can recall following Matsuda's steady stride along the steel bridge at Nishizuru, mopping the sweat from my face and wishing my companion would walk more slowly. Matsuda was dressed that day in an elegant white summer jacket and, as ever, wore his hat slanted down stylishly. For all his pace, his strides had an effortless quality with no suggestion of hurry. And when he paused, half-way across the bridge, I saw he did not seem even to be suffering from the heat.

'You get an interesting view from up here,' he remarked. 'You agree, Ono?'

The view below us was framed by two factory plants looming one to our right, the other to our left. Wedged in between was a dense muddle of roofs, some of the cheap shingled variety, others improvised out of corrugated metals. The Nishizuru district still has today a certain reputation as a deprived area, but in those days, things were infinitely worse. Viewed from the bridge, a stranger may well have assumed that community to be some derelict site half-way to demolition were it not for the many small figures, visible on closer inspection, moving busily around the houses like ants swarming around stones.

'Look down there, Ono,' Matsuda said. 'There are more and more places in our city like this. Only two or three years ago, this was not such a bad place. But now it's growing into a shanty district. More and more people become poor, Ono, and they are obliged to leave their houses in the countryside to join their fellow sufferers in places like this.'

'How terrible,' I said. 'It makes one want to do something for them.'

Matsuda smiled at me – one of his superior smiles which always made me feel uncomfortable and foolish. 'Well-meaning sentiments,' he said, turning back to the view. 'We all utter them. In every walk of life. Meanwhile, places like these grow everywhere like a bad fungus. Take a deep breath, Ono. Even from here, you can smell the sewage.'

'I'd noticed an odour. Is it really coming from down there?'

Matsuda did not reply, but continued to look down at that shanty community with a strange smile on his face. Then he said:

'Politicians and businessmen rarely see places like this. At least if they do, they stand at a safe distance, as we are now. I doubt if many politicians or businessmen have taken a walk down there. Come to that, I doubt if many artists have either.'

Noticing the challenge in his voice, I said:

'I wouldn't object if it won't make us late for our appointment.'

'On the contrary, we will save ourselves a kilometre or two by cutting through down there.'

Matsuda had been correct in supposing the odour derived from the sewers of that community. As we climbed down to the foot of the steel bridge and began making our way through a series of narrow alleys, the smell grew ever stronger until it became quite nauseous. There was no longer a trace of wind to combat the heat, the only movement in the air around us being the perpetual buzzing of flies. Again, I found myself struggling to keep up with Matsuda's strides, but this time felt no desire for him to slow down.

On either side of us were what might have been stalls at some marketplace, closed down for the day, but which in fact constituted individual households, partitioned from the alleyway sometimes only by a cloth curtain. Old people sat in some of the doorways, and as we went past gave interested, though never hostile, stares; small children appeared to be coming and going in all directions, while cats too seemed forever to be scurrying away from around our feet. We walked on, dodging blankets and washing hung out along coarse pieces of string; past crying babies, barking dogs and neighbours chatting amiably across the alleyway to each other, seemingly from behind closed curtains. After a while, I grew increasingly aware of the open-sewer ditches dug on either side of the narrow path we were walking. There were flies hovering all along their length and as I continued to follow Matsuda, I had the distinct feeling the space between the ditches was growing more and more narrow, until it was as though we were balancing along a fallen tree trunk.

Eventually we came to a kind of yard where a crowd of shanty huts closed off the way ahead. But Matsuda pointed to a gap between two of the huts through which was visible an open piece of wasteground.

'If we cut across there,' he said, 'we'll come up behind Kogane Street.'

Near the entrance of the passage Matsuda had indicated, I noticed three small boys bowed over something on the ground, prodding at it with sticks. As we approached, they spun round with scowls on their faces and although I saw nothing, something in their manner told me they were torturing some animal. Matsuda must have drawn the same conclusion, for he said to me as we walked past: 'Well, they have little else to amuse themselves with around here.'

I gave those boys little further thought at the time. Then some days later, that image of the three of them, turning towards us with scowls on their faces, brandishing their sticks, standing there amidst all that squalor, returned to me with some vividness, and I used it as the central image of 'Complacency'. But I might point out that when the Tortoise stole a look at my unfinished painting that morning, the three boys he saw would have differed from their models in one or two important respects. For although they still stood in front of a squalid shanty hut, and their clothes were the same rags the original boys wore, the scowls on their faces would not have been guilty, defensive scowls of little criminals caught in the act; rather, they would have worn the manly scowls of samurai warriors ready to fight. It is no coincidence, furthermore, that the boys in my picture held their sticks in classic kendo stances.

Above the heads of these three boys, the Tortoise would have seen the painting fading into a second image – that of three fat, well-dressed men, sitting in a comfortable bar laughing together. The looks on their faces seem decadent; perhaps they are exchanging jokes about their mistresses or some such matter. These two contrasting images are moulded together within the coastline of the Japanese islands. Down the right-hand margin, in bold red characters, is the word 'Complacency'; down the left-hand side, in smaller characters, is the declaration: 'But the young are ready to fight for their dignity.'

When I describe this early and no doubt unsophisticated work, certain of its features may perhaps strike you as familiar. For it is possible you are acquainted with my painting, 'Eyes to the Horizon' which, as a print in the thirties, achieved a certain fame and influence throughout this city. 'Eyes to the Horizon' was indeed a reworking of 'Complacency', though with such differences as might be expected given the passage of years between the two. The later painting, you may recall, also employed two contrasting images merging into one another, bound by the coastline of Japan; the upper image was again that of three well-dressed men conferring, but this time they wore nervous expressions, looking to each other for initiative. And these faces, I need not remind you, resembled those of three prominent politicians. For the lower, more dominant image, the three poverty-stricken boys had become stern-faced soldiers; two of them held bayoneted rifles, flanking an officer who held out his sword, pointing the way forward, west towards Asia. Behind them, there was no longer a backdrop of poverty; simply the military flag of the rising sun. The word 'Complacency' down the right-hand margin had been replaced by 'Eyes to the Horizon!' and on the left-hand side, the message, 'No time for cowardly talking. Japan must go forward.'

Of course, if you are new to this city, it is possible you will not have come across this work. But I do not think it an exaggeration to say that a great many of those living here before the war would be familiar with it, for it did receive much praise at the time for its vigorous brush technique and, particularly, its powerful use of colour. But I am fully aware, of course, that 'Eyes to the Horizon', whatever its artistic merits, is a painting whose sentiments are now outdated. Indeed, I would be the first to admit that those same sentiments are perhaps worthy of condemnation. I am not one of those who are afraid to admit to the shortcomings of past achievements.

But I did not wish to discuss 'Eyes to the Horizon'. I mention it here only because of its obvious relationship to that earlier painting, and I suppose, to acknowledge the impact my meeting Matsuda had on my subsequent career. I had begun to see Matsuda regularly some weeks prior to that morning in the kitchen when the Tortoise had made his discovery. It is, I suppose, a measure of the appeal his ideas had for me that I continued to meet him, for as I recall, I did not at first take much of a liking to him. Indeed, most of our earlier meetings would end with our becoming extremely antagonistic towards one another. I remember one evening, for instance, not long after that day I followed him through the poverty of Nishizuru, going with him to a bar somewhere in the city centre. I do not recall the name or the whereabouts of the bar, but I remember it vividly as a dark, dirty place, frequented by what looked to be the city's low life. I felt apprehensive as soon as I walked in, but Matsuda seemed to be familiar with the place, saluting to some men playing cards around a table, before leading me to an alcove containing a small, unoccupied table.

My apprehension was not eased when shortly after we had sat down, two rough-looking men, both fairly drunk, came staggering into the alcove, wishing to engage us in conversation. Matsuda told them quite flatly to go away, and I fully expected trouble, but something about my companion seemed to unnerve the men, and they left us without comment.

After that, we sat drinking and conversing for some time, and before long, I recall, our exchanges had become abrasive. At one point I remember saying to him:

'No doubt, we artists may at times deserve mockery from the likes of you. But I'm afraid you're mistaken in assuming we're all so naïve about the world.'

Matsuda laughed and said:

'But you must remember, Ono, I come across many artists. You are on the whole an astonishingly decadent crowd. Often with no more than a child's knowledge of the affairs of this world.'

I was about to protest, but Matsuda continued: 'Take for instance, Ono, this scheme of yours. The one you were proposing so earnestly just now. It's very touching, but if I may say so, displays all the naïveté typical of you artists.'

'I fail to see why my idea is so worthy of your mockery. But then I obviously made a mistake in assuming you felt concern for the poor of this city.'

'No need for such childish jibes. You know very well my concern. But let's consider your little scheme for a moment. Let's suppose the unlikely occurs and your teacher is sympathetic. So then all of you at your villa will spend a week, perhaps two, producing – what? – twenty paintings? Thirty at the most. There seems little point in producing more, you won't sell more than ten or eleven in any case. What will you do then, Ono? Wander the poor areas of this city with a little purse of coins you've raised from all this hard work? Give a sen to each poor person you meet?'

'Forgive me, Matsuda, but I must repeat – you're quite wrong to assume me so naïve. I wasn't for a moment suggesting the exhibition be confined simply to Mori-san's group. I'm fully aware of the scale of the poverty we're seeking to alleviate, and this is why I'm coming to you with this suggestion. Your Okada-Shingen Society is ably placed to develop such a scheme. Large exhibitions held regularly throughout the city, attracting ever more artists, would bring significant relief to these people.'

'I'm sorry, Ono,' Matsuda said, smiling and shaking his head, 'but I fear I was correct in my assumption after all. As a breed, you artists are desperately naïve.' He leaned back in his seat and gave a sigh. The surface of our table was covered in cigarette ash and Matsuda was thoughtfully sweeping patterns in it with the edge of an empty matchbox left by previous occupants. 'There's a certain kind of artist these days,' he went on, 'whose greatest talent lies in hiding away from the real world. Unfortunately, such artists appear to be in dominance at present, and you, Ono, have come under the sway of one of them. Don't look so angry, it's true. Your knowledge of the world is like a child's. I doubt, for instance, if you could even tell me who Karl Marx was.'

I gave him what must have been a sulky look, but said nothing. He gave a laugh and said: 'You see? But don't be too upset. Most of your colleagues know no better.'

'Don't be ridiculous. Of course I know of Karl Marx.'

'Why, I'm sorry, Ono. Perhaps I did underestimate you. Please, tell me about Marx.'

I shrugged and said: 'I believe he led the Russian revolution.'

'Then what about Lenin, Ono? Was he perhaps Marx's second-in-command?'

'A colleague of some kind.' I saw Matsuda was grinning again, and so said quickly, before he could speak: 'In any case, you're being preposterous. These are the concerns of some far-away country. I'm talking about the poor here in our own city.'

'Indeed, Ono, indeed. But there again, you see, you know very little about anything. You were quite correct in assuming the Okada-Shingen Society was concerned to wake up artists and introduce them to the real world. But I have misled you if I ever suggested our society wished to be turned into a large begging bowl. We're not interested in charity.'

'I fail to see what there is to object to in a little charity. And if at the same time it opens the eyes of us decadent artists, then so much the better, I would have thought.'

'Your eyes are indeed far from open, Ono, if you believe a little good-hearted charity can help the poor of our country. The truth is, Japan is headed for crisis. We are in the hands of greedy businessmen and weak politicians. Such people will see to it poverty grows every day. Unless, that is, we, the emerging generation, take action. But I'm no political agitator, Ono. My concern is with art. And with artists like you. Talented young artists, not yet irreversibly blinkered by that enclosed little world you all inhabit. The Okada-Shingen exists to help the likes of you open your eyes and produce work of genuine value for these difficult times.'

'Forgive me, Matsuda, but it strikes me it's you who are in fact the naïve one. An artist's concern is to capture beauty wherever he finds it. But however skilfully he may come to do this, he will have little influence on the sort of matters you talk of. Indeed, if the Okada-Shingen is as you claim it is, then it seems to me ill-conceived indeed. It seems to be founded on a naïve mistake about what art can and cannot do.'

'You know full well, Ono, we do not see things so simply. The fact is, the Okada-Shingen does not exist in isolation. There are young men like us in all walks of life – in politics, in the military – who think the same way. We are the emerging generation. Together, it is within our capability to achieve something of real value. It just so happens that some of us care deeply about art and wish to see it responding to the world of today. The truth is, Ono, in times like these, when people are getting poorer, and children are growing more hungry and sick all around you, it is simply not enough for an artist to hide away somewhere, perfecting pictures of courtesans. I can see you're angry with me, and even now you're searching for some way to come back at me. But I mean well, Ono. I hope later on you'll think carefully about these things. For you, above all, are someone of immense talent.'

'Well, do tell me then, Matsuda. How can we decadent foolish artists help bring about your political revolution?'

To my annoyance, Matsuda was once more smiling disparagingly across the table. 'Revolution? Really, Ono! The communists want a revolution. We want nothing of the sort. Quite the opposite, in fact. We wish for a restoration. We simply ask that his Imperial Majesty the Emperor be restored to his rightful place as head of our state.'

'But our Emperor is precisely that already.'

'Really, Ono. So naïve and confused.' His voice, though it remained, as ever, perfectly calm, seemed at this point to grow harder. 'Our Emperor is our rightful leader, and yet what in reality has become of things? Power has been grasped from him by these businessmen and their politicians. Listen, Ono, Japan is no longer a backward country of peasant farmers. We are now a mighty nation, capable of matching any of the Western nations. In the Asian hemisphere, Japan stands like a giant amidst cripples and dwarfs. And yet we allow our people to grow more and more desperate, our little children to die of malnutrition. Meanwhile, the businessmen get richer and the politicians forever make excuses and chatter. Can you imagine any of the Western powers allowing such a situation? They would surely have taken action long ago.'

'Action? What sort of action do you refer to, Matsuda?'

'It's time for us to forge an empire as powerful and wealthy as those of the British and the French. We must use our strength to expand abroad. The time is now well due for Japan to take her rightful place amongst the world powers. Believe me, Ono, we have the means to do so, but have yet to discover the will. And we must rid ourselves of these businessmen and politicians. Then the military will be answerable only to his Imperial Majesty the Emperor.' Then he gave a small laugh and turned his gaze back down to the patterns he was weaving in the cigarette ash. 'But this is largely for others to worry over,' he said. 'The likes of us, Ono, we must concern ourselves with art.'

It is my belief, though, that the reason for the Tortoise's upset in the disused kitchen two or three weeks later had not so much to do with these issues I discussed with Matsuda that night; the Tortoise would not have had the perception to have seen so far into that unfinished painting of mine. All he would have recognized was that it represented a blatant disregard for Mori-san's priorities; abandoned had been the school's collective endeavour to capture the fragile lantern light of the pleasure world; bold calligraphy had been introduced to complement the visual impact; and above all, no doubt, the Tortoise would have been shocked to observe that my technique made extensive use of the hard outline – a traditional enough method, as you will know, but one whose rejection was fundamental to Mori-san's teaching.

Whatever the reasons for his outrage, I knew after that morning I could no longer hide my rapidly developing ideas from those around me, and that it was only a matter of time before our teacher himself came to hear of it all. Thus, by the time I had that conversation with Mori-san inside the pavilion at Takami Gardens, I had turned over in my mind many times what I might say to him, and was firmly resolved not to let myself down.

It was a week or so after that morning in the kitchen. Mori-san and I had spent the afternoon in the city on some errand – perhaps to select and order our materials, I do not remember. What I do recall is that as we went about our business, Mori-san did not behave in any way oddly towards me. Then, with the evening drawing in, finding ourselves with a little time before our train, we climbed the steep steps behind Yotsugawa Station up to the Takami Gardens.

In those days there stood up on Takami Gardens a most pleasing pavilion, just on the rim of the hill overlooking the area – not far, in fact, from where the peace memorial stands today. The most noticeably attractive feature of the pavilion was the way the eaves of its elegant roof were hung all the way round with lanterns – although on that particular night, as I recall, the lanterns were all unlit as we approached. Stepping in under the roof, the pavilion was as spacious as a large room, but since it was not enclosed on any side, only the arched posts supporting the roof broke one's view out over the district below.

Quite possibly, that evening with Mori-san was the occasion I first discovered that pavilion. It was to remain a favourite spot for me over the years, until it was eventually destroyed during the war, and I often took my own pupils there whenever we happened to be passing that way. Indeed, I believe it was in that same pavilion, just before the start of the war, that I was to have my last conversation with Kuroda, the most gifted of my pupils.

In any case, that first evening I followed Mori-san inside it, I recall the sky had become a pale crimson colour and lights were coming on amidst the muddle of roofs still visible down below in the gloom. Mori-san took a few further steps towards the view, then leaning a shoulder against a post, looked up at the sky with some satisfaction and said without turning to me:

'Ono, there are some matches and tapers in our kerchief. Kindly light these lanterns. The effect, I imagine, will be most interesting.'

As I made my way around the pavilion, lighting lantern after lantern, the gardens around us, which had become still and silent, steadily faded into darkness. All the while, I continued to glance towards the silhouette of Mori-san outlined against the sky, gazing out thoughtfully at the view. I had lit perhaps half of the lanterns when I heard him say:

'So then, Ono, what is this matter troubling you so much?'

'I'm sorry, Sensei?'

'You mentioned earlier today, there was something troubling you.'

I gave a small laugh as I reached up towards a lantern.

'Just a small thing, Sensei. I wouldn't bother Sensei with it, but then I am not sure what to make of it. The fact is, two days ago, I discovered that certain of my paintings had been removed from where I always store them in the old kitchen.'

Mori-san remained silent for a moment. Then he said:

'And what did the others have to say about this?'

'I asked them, but no one seemed to know anything. Or at least, no one seemed willing to tell me.'

'So what did you conclude, Ono? Is there some conspiracy against you?'

'Well, as a matter of fact, Sensei, the others do appear anxious to avoid my company. Indeed, I have been unable to have a single conversation with any of them over these past few days. When I enter a room, people go silent or else leave altogether.'

He made no comment on this, and when I glanced towards him, he appeared to be still absorbed by the setting sky. I was in the process of lighting another lantern when I heard him say:

'Your paintings are presently in my possession. I'm sorry if I caused you alarm by taking them. It just so happened I had a little spare time the other day and thought it a good opportunity to catch up on your recent work. You appeared to be out somewhere at the time. I suppose I should have told you when you returned, Ono. My apologies.'

'Why, not at all, Sensei. I'm most grateful you should take such an interest in my work.'

'But it's only natural I should take interest. You are my most accomplished pupil. I have invested years nurturing your talent.'

'Of course, Sensei. I cannot begin to estimate what I owe you.'

Neither of us spoke for a few moments, while I continued to light lanterns. Then I paused and said:

'I am very relieved no harm has come to my paintings. I should have known there was some simple explanation of this kind. I can now put my mind at rest.'

Mori-san said nothing to this, and from what I could make of his silhouette, he did not take his eyes from the view. It occurred to me he had not heard me, so I said a little more loudly:

'I am glad I can put my mind at rest regarding the safety of my paintings.'

'Yes, Ono,' Mori-san said, as though startled out of some far-away thoughts. 'I had a little spare time on my hands. So I had someone go and fetch me your recent work.'

'It was foolish of me to have worried. I'm glad the paintings are safe.'

He did not speak for some time so that I again thought he had not heard me. But then he said: 'I was a little surprised by what I saw. You seem to be exploring curious avenues.'

Of course, he may well not have used that precise phrase, 'exploring curious avenues'. For it occurs to me that expression was one I myself tended to use frequently in later years and it may well be that I am remembering my own words to Kuroda on that later occasion in that same pavilion. But then again, I believe Mori-san did at times refer to 'exploring avenues'; in fact, this is probably another example of my inheriting a characteristic from my former teacher. In any case, I recall I did not respond other than to give a self-conscious laugh and reach for another lantern. Then I heard him saying:

'It's no bad thing that a young artist experiment a little. Amongst other things, he is able to get some of his more superficial interests out of his system that way. Then he can return to more serious work with more commitment than ever.' Then, after a pause, he muttered as though to himself: 'No, it's no bad thing to experiment. It's all part of being young. It's no bad thing at all.'

'Sensei,' I said, 'I feel strongly that my recent work is the finest I have yet done.'

'It's no bad thing, no bad thing at all. But then again, one shouldn't spend too much time with such experiments. One can become like someone who travels too much. Best return to serious work before too long.'

I waited to see if he would say anything more. After a few moments, I said: 'I was no doubt foolish to worry so much for the safety of those paintings. But you see, Sensei, I am more proud of them than anything else I have done. All the same, I should have guessed there would be some such simple explanation.'

Mori-san remained silent. When I glanced at him past the lantern I was lighting, it was difficult to tell whether he was pondering my words or thinking about something else altogether. There was a strange mixture of light in the pavilion as the sky continued to set and I lit more and more lanterns. But Mori-san's figure remained in silhouette, leaning against a post, his back to me.

'Incidentally, Ono,' he said, eventually, 'I was told there were one or two other paintings you've completed recently that were not with those I have now.'

'Quite possibly, there are one or two I did not store with the others.'

'Ah. And no doubt these are the very paintings you are most fond of.'

I did not reply to this. Then Mori-san went on:

'Perhaps when we return, Ono, you will bring me these other paintings. I would be most interested to see them.'

I thought for a moment, then said: 'I would, of course, be most grateful for Sensei's opinions of them. However, I am not at all certain as to where I left them.'

'But you will endeavour to find them, I trust.'

'I will, Sensei. In the meantime, I will perhaps relieve Sensei of the other paintings to which he was so kind as to give his attention. No doubt they are cluttering up his quarters, so I shall remove them as soon as we return.'

'No need to bother with those paintings, Ono. It will be sufficient if you find the remaining ones and bring them to me.'

'I regret, Sensei, that I will not be able to find the remaining paintings.'

'I see, Ono.' He gave a tired sigh, and I could see him once again gazing up at the sky. 'So you do not think you will be able to bring me those paintings of yours.'

'No, Sensei. I fear not.'

'I see. Of course, you have considered your future in the event of your leaving my patronage.'

'It had been my hope that Sensei would understand my position and continue to support me in pursuing my career.'

He remained silent, so eventually I went on:

'Sensei, it would cause me the greatest pain to leave the villa. These past several years have been the happiest and most valuable of my life. My colleagues I look upon as brothers. And as for Sensei himself, why, I can hardly begin to estimate what I owe him. I would beg you to look once more at my new paintings and reconsider them. Perhaps, in fact, Sensei will allow me when we return to explain my intentions in each picture.'

He still gave no sign of having heard me. So I continued:

'I have learnt many things over these past years. I have learnt much in contemplating the world of pleasure, and recognizing its fragile beauty. But I now feel it is time for me to progress to other things. Sensei, it is my belief that in such troubled times as these, artists must learn to value something more tangible than those pleasurable things that disappear with the morning light. It is not necessary that artists always occupy a decadent and enclosed world. My conscience, Sensei, tells me I cannot remain forever an artist of the floating world.'

With that, I turned my attention back to the lanterns. After a few moments, Mori-san said:

'You have been for some time now my most accomplished pupil. It will be a matter of some pain to me to see you leave. Let us say, then, that you have three days to bring me those remaining paintings. You will bring those to me, then turn your mind back to more proper concerns.'

'As I have already said, Sensei, it is to my deep regret that I will be unable to bring you those paintings.'

Mori-san made a sound as though he were laughing to himself. Then he said: 'As you point out yourself, Ono, these are troubled times. All the more so for a young artist, practically unknown and without resources. If you were less talented, I would fear for your future after leaving me. But you are a clever fellow. No doubt you have made arrangements.'

'As a matter of fact, I have made no arrangements whatsoever. The villa has been my home for so long, I never seriously contemplated it ceasing to be so.'

'Is that so. Well, as I say, Ono, were you less talented, there would be cause for worry. But you are a clever young man.' I saw Mori-san's silhouette turn to face me. 'You will no doubt succeed in finding work illustrating magazines and comic books. Perhaps you will even manage to join a firm like the one you were employed by when you first came to me. Of course, it will mean the end of your development as a serious artist, but then no doubt you've taken all this into account.'

These may sound unnecessarily vindictive words for a teacher to use to a pupil whose admiration he knows he still commands. But then again, when a master painter has given so much in time and resources to a certain pupil, when furthermore he has allowed that pupil's name to be associated in public with his own, it is perhaps understandable, if not entirely excusable, that the teacher lose for a moment his sense of proportion and react in ways he may later regret. And though the manoeuvrings over the possession of the paintings will no doubt appear petty, it is surely understandable if a teacher who has actually supplied most of the paints and materials should forget in such a moment that his pupil has any right whatever over his own work.

For all that, it is clear that such arrogance and possessiveness on the part of a teacher – however renowned he may be – is to be regretted. From time to time, I still turn over in my mind that cold winter's morning and the smell of burning growing ever stronger in my nostrils. It was the winter before the outbreak of war and I was standing anxiously at the door of Kuroda's house – a shabby little affair he used to rent in the Nakamachi area. The burning smell, I could tell, originated from somewhere within the house, from where also came the sound of a woman sobbing. I pulled the bell rope repeatedly and shouted for someone to come and receive me, but there was no response. Eventually I decided to let myself in, but as I pulled back the outer door, a uniformed policeman appeared in the entryway.

'What do you want?' he demanded.

'I came looking for Mr Kuroda. He is home?'

'The occupant has been taken to police headquarters for questioning.'

'Questioning?'

'I advise you to go home,' the officer said. 'Or else we'll be wanting to start checking on you too. We're interested now in all close associates of the occupant.'

'But why? Has Mr Kuroda committed any crime?'

'No one wants his sort around. If you don't go on your way, we'll have you in for questioning too.'

Inside the house, the woman – Kuroda's mother, I assumed – continued to sob. I could hear someone shouting something at her.

'Where is the officer in charge?' I asked.

'On your way. You want to be arrested?'

'Before we go any further,' I said, 'let me explain that my name is Ono.' The officer showed no recognition, so I continued a little uncertainly: 'I am the man on whose information you have been brought here. I am Masuji Ono, the artist and member of the Cultural Committee of the Interior Department. Indeed, I am an official adviser to the Committee of Unpatriotic Activities. I believe there's been some sort of mistake here and I would like to speak with whoever is in charge.'

The officer looked at me suspiciously for a moment, then turned and disappeared into the house. Before long, he came back and gestured for me to step up.

As I followed him through Kuroda's house, I saw everywhere the contents of cupboards and drawers emptied out over the floor. Some books, I noticed, had been piled up and tied into bundles, while in the main room, the tatami had been lifted and an officer was investigating the floorboards beneath with a torch. From behind a closed partition, I could hear more clearly Kuroda's mother sobbing and an officer shouting questions at her.

I was led out to the veranda at the back of the house. In the middle of the small yard another uniformed officer and a man in plain clothes were standing around a bonfire. The plain-clothes man turned and came a few steps towards me.

'Mr Ono?' he asked, quite respectfully.

The officer who had led me in seemed to sense his earlier rudeness had been inappropriate and quickly turned back into the house.

'What has happened to Mr Kuroda?'

'Taken for questioning, Mr Ono. We'll take care of him, don't you worry.'

I stared past him at the fire, now almost burnt out. The uniformed officer was poking the pile with a stick.

'Did you have authorization to burn those paintings?' I asked.

'It's our policy to destroy any offensive material which won't be needed as evidence. We've selected a good enough sample. The rest of this trash we're just burning.'

'I had no idea', I said, 'something like this would happen. I merely suggested to the committee someone come round and give Mr Kuroda a talking-to for his own good.' I stared again at the smouldering pile in the middle of the yard. 'It was quite unnecessary to burn those. There were many fine works amongst them.'

'Mr Ono, we're grateful for your help. But now the investigations have been started, you must leave them in the hands of the appropriate authorities. We'll see to it your Mr Kuroda is treated fairly.'

He smiled, and turning back to the fire, said something to the uniformed officer. The latter poked the fire again and said something under his breath which sounded like: 'Unpatriotic trash.'

I remained on the veranda, watching with unbelieving eyes. Eventually, the plain-clothes officer turned to me again and said: 'Mr Ono, I suggest you return home now.'

'Things have gone much too far,' I said. 'And why are you interrogating Mrs Kuroda? What has she to do with anything?'

'This is a police matter now, Mr Ono. It doesn't concern you any longer.'

'Things have gone much too far. I intend to discuss this with Mr Ubukata. Indeed, I may well take it straight up to Mr Saburi himself.'

The plain-clothes man called to someone in the house and the officer who had answered the door to me appeared at my side.

'Thank Mr Ono for his help and show him out,' the

plain-clothes man said. Then as he turned back to the fire, he gave a sudden cough. 'Bad paintings make bad smoke,' he said with a grin, beating at the air about his face.

But this is all of limited relevance here. I believe I was recalling the events of that day last month when Setsuko was down on her short visit; in fact, I was recounting how Taro had got us all laughing around the supper table with his anecdotes about his work colleagues.

As I remember, supper continued to proceed in a most satisfactory manner. I could not, however, avoid some discomfort in observing Ichiro whenever Noriko poured out sake. For the first few times, he would glance across the table at me with a conspiratorial smile, which I did my best to return in as neutral a way as possible. But then as the meal progressed, and sake continued to be poured, he ceased to look at me, but would stare crossly at his aunt as she refilled our cups.

Taro had told us several more amusing stories about his colleagues, when Setsuko said to him:

'You make such fun, Taro-san. But I learn from Noriko that morale is very high at your company just now. Surely, it must be most stimulating to work in such an atmosphere.'

At this, Taro's manner became suddenly very earnest. 'It is indeed, Setsuko-san,' he said, nodding. 'The changes we made after the war are now beginning to bear fruit at all levels of the company. We feel very optimistic about the future. Within the next ten years, provided we all do our best, KNC should be a name recognized not just all over Japan but all over the world.'

'How splendid. And Noriko was telling me your branch director is a very kindly man. That too must make a big difference to morale.'

'You're indeed right. But then Mr Hayasaka is not only a kindly man, he is someone of the greatest ability and vision. I can assure you, Setsuko-san, to work for an incompetent superior, however kindly, can be a demoralizing experience. We are very fortunate to have someone like Mr Hayasaka to lead us.'

'Indeed, Suichi too is very fortunate in that he has a very capable superior.'

'Is that so, Setsuko-san? But then I would expect as much of a company like Nippon Electrics. Only the best sort of people would hold responsibility in such a firm.'

'We are so fortunate that seems to be the case. But I am sure it is equally true at KNC, Taro-san. Suichi always speaks highly of KNC.'

'Excuse me, Taro,' I put in at this point. 'Of course, I'm sure you have every reason to be optimistic at KNC. But I've been meaning to ask you, is it in your opinion entirely for the good that so many sweeping changes were made at your firm after the war? I hear there is hardly any of the old management left.'

My son-in-law smiled thoughtfully, then said: 'I appreciate very much Father's concern. Youth and vigour alone will not always produce the best results. But in all frankness, Father, a complete overhaul was called for. We needed new leaders with a new approach appropriate to the world of today.'

'Of course, of course. And I've no doubt your new leaders are the most capable of men. But tell me, Taro, don't you worry at times we might be a little too hasty in following the Americans? I would be the first to agree many of the old ways must now be erased for ever, but don't you think sometimes some good things are being thrown out with the bad? Indeed, sometimes Japan has come to look like a small child learning from a strange adult.'

'Father is very right. At times, I'm sure, we have been a little hasty. But by and large, the Americans have an immense amount to teach us. Just in these few years, for instance, we Japanese have already come a long way in understanding such things as democracy and individual rights. Indeed,

Father, I have a feeling Japan has finally established a foundation on which to build a brilliant future. This is why firms like ours can look forward with the greatest confidence.'

'Indeed, Taro-san,' Setsuko said. 'Suichi has just that same feeling. He has expressed on a number of occasions recently his opinion that after four years of confusion, our country has finally set its sights on the future.'

Although my daughter had addressed this remark to Taro, I had the distinct impression it had been made for my benefit. Taro too seemed to take it that way, for rather than reply to Setsuko, he continued:

'In fact, Father, just the other week I attended a reunion dinner of my school graduation year and for the first time since the surrender, all those present from every walk of life were expressing optimism for the future. It is then by no means just at KNC there is a feeling things are coming right. And while I fully understand Father's worries, I'm confident that by and large the lessons of these past years have been good ones and will lead us all on to a splendid future. But perhaps I am to be corrected, Father.'

'Not at all, not at all,' I said, and gave him a smile. 'As you say, no doubt your generation has a splendid future. And you are all so confident. I can only wish you the best.'

My son-in-law seemed about to respond to this, but just then, Ichiro reached across the table and tapped the sake flask with his finger, as he had done once before. Taro turned to him, saying: 'Ah, Ichiro-san. Just who we needed for our discussions. Tell us, what do you think you'll be when you grow up?'

My grandson continued to regard the sake flask for a moment, then glanced over towards me with a sullen look. His mother touched his arm, whispering to him: 'Ichiro, Uncle Taro's asking you. You tell him what you want to be.'

'President of Nippon Electrics!' Ichiro declared loudly.

We all laughed.

'Now are you sure of that, Ichiro-san?' Taro asked. 'You don't instead wish to lead us at KNC?'

'Nippon Electrics is the best company!'

We all laughed again.

'A great shame for us,' Taro remarked. 'Ichiro-san is just who we'll need at KNC in a few years.'

This exchange seemed to take Ichiro's mind off the sake, and from then on, he seemed to enjoy himself, joining in loudly whenever the adults laughed at something. Only towards the very end of our meal did he ask in a quite disinterested voice:

'Is the sake all finished now?'

'All gone,' Noriko said. 'Would Ichiro-san like more orange juice?'

Ichiro refused this offer in a well-mannered way, and turned back to Taro, who had been explaining something to him. For all that, I could imagine his disappointment and felt a wave of irritation at Setsuko for not being a little more understanding of her little boy's feelings.

I got my chance to talk alone with Ichiro an hour or so later when I went into the small spare room of the apartment to say good-night to him. The light was still on, but Ichiro was under the quilt, on his front, a cheek pressed against his pillow. When I turned off the light, I discovered the blinds did not prevent light from the opposite apartment block coming into the room to throw shadowy bars across the walls and ceiling. From the next room came the sounds of my daughters laughing over something, and as I knelt down beside Ichiro's quilt he whispered:

'Oji, is Aunt Noriko drunk?'

'I don't think so, Ichiro. She's just laughing at something, that's all.'

'She might be a little bit drunk. Don't you think, Oji?'

'Well, perhaps. Just a little. There's no harm in that.'

'Women can't handle sake, can they, Oji?' he said, and giggled into his pillow.

I gave a laugh, then said to him: 'You know, Ichiro, there's no need to be upset about the sake tonight. It really doesn't matter. Soon you'll be older, and then you'll be able to drink sake as much as you like.'

I rose and went to the window to see if the blinds could not be made more effective. I opened and shut them a few times, but the slats remained sufficiently separated so that I could always see the lighted windows of the block opposite.

'No, Ichiro, it's really nothing to get upset about.'

For a moment, my grandson gave no response. Then I heard his voice say behind me: 'Oji's not to worry.'

'Oh? Now what do you mean by that, Ichiro?'

'Oji's not to worry. Because if he worries, he won't get to sleep. And if old people don't sleep, they get ill.'

'I see. Very well then, Ichiro. Oji promises not to worry. But you're not to be upset either. Because really, there's nothing to be getting upset about.'

Ichiro remained silent. I opened and closed the blinds again.

'But then, of course,' I said, 'if Ichiro had actually insisted on sake tonight, Oji was ready to step in and see to it he got some. But as it was, I think we were right to let the women have their way this time. It's not worth getting them upset over such little things.'

'Sometimes at home,' Ichiro said, 'Father wants to do something and Mother tells him it's not allowed. Sometimes, even Father's no match for Mother.'

'Is that so,' I said, with a laugh.

'So Oji's not to worry.'

'There's nothing for either of us to worry about, Ichiro.' I turned away from the window and knelt down again beside his quilt. 'Now you try and fall asleep.'

'Is Oji staying the night?'

'No, Oji's going back to his own house soon.'

'Why can't Oji stay here too?'

'There's not enough room here, Ichiro. Oji has a large house all to himself, remember.'

'Will Oji come to say goodbye at the station tomorrow?'

'Of course, Ichiro. I'll do that. And no doubt, you'll be down to visit again before long.'

'Oji's not to worry he couldn't make Mother give me sake.'

'You seem to be growing up very fast, Ichiro,' I said, laughing. 'You'll be a fine man when you're grown. Perhaps you really will be head of Nippon Electrics. Or something just as grand. Now, let's keep quiet for a while and see if you fall asleep.'

I went on sitting beside him for several more moments, giving quiet replies whenever he spoke. And I believe it was during those moments, as I waited in that darkened room for my grandson to fall asleep, listening to the occasional burst of laughter from the neighbouring room, that I began turning over in my mind the conversation I had had that morning with Setsuko in Kawabe Park. That was probably the first opportunity I had had to do so, and until that point, it had not really occurred to me to be so irritated by Setsuko's words. But by the time I left my sleeping grandson to rejoin the others in the main room, I believe I had become quite annoyed with my elder daughter, and this no doubt accounts for my saying to Taro, not long after I had sat down:

'You know, it's odd when one thinks about it. Your father and I must have been acquainted for over sixteen years, and yet it's only over this past year we've become such good friends.'

'Indeed,' said my son-in-law, 'but I suppose it's often that way. One always has so many neighbours one does no more than exchange good mornings with. A great pity when you think about it.'

'But then of course,' I said, 'as regards Dr Saito and myself, it wasn't simply that we were neighbours. Connected as we both were with the art world, we knew of each other by reputation. All the more pity then that your father and I didn't make more effort to be friends from the beginning. Don't you think so, Taro?'

As I said this, I gave a quick glance towards Setsuko to make sure she was listening.

'A great pity indeed,' Taro said. 'But at least you had the chance to become friends in the end.'

'But what I mean, Taro, is that it's all the more pity since we knew each of other's reputations in the art world all that time.'

'Yes, a great pity indeed. One would think the knowledge that a neighbour was also a distinguished colleague would lead to more intimate relations. But then I suppose, what with busy schedules and the next thing, this is too often not the case.'

I glanced with some satisfaction towards Setsuko, but my daughter showed no sign at all of registering the significance of Taro's words. It is possible, of course, that she was not really attending; my guess, though, is that Setsuko had indeed understood, but was too proud to return my glance, confronted as she was with proof that she had been quite mistaken in making her insinuations that morning in Kawabe Park.

We had been walking down the wide central avenue of the park at an easy pace, admiring the autumnal trees lined on either side of us. We had been comparing our impressions on how Noriko was taking to her new life, and had agreed that to all appearances, she was very happy indeed.

'It's all very gratifying,' I was saying. 'Her future was becoming a grave worry to me, but now everything looks very good for her. Taro is an admirable man. One could hardly have hoped for a better match.'

'It seems strange to think', Setsuko said with a smile, 'it was only a year ago we were all so worried for her.'

'It's all very gratifying. And you know, Setsuko, I'm grateful to you for your part in it all. You were a great support to your sister when things weren't going so well.'

'On the contrary, I could do so little, being so far away.'

'And of course,' I said, with a laugh, 'it was you who

warned me last year. "Precautionary steps" – you remember that, Setsuko? As you see, I didn't ignore your advice.'

'I'm sorry, Father, what advice was this?'

'Now Setsuko, there's no need to be so tactful. I'm quite prepared now to acknowledge there are certain aspects to my career I have no cause to be proud of. Indeed, I acknowledged as much during the negotiations, just as you suggested.'

'I'm sorry, I'm not at all clear what Father is referring to.'

'Noriko hasn't told you about the *miai*? Well, I made sure that evening there'd be no obstacles to her happiness on account of my career. I dare say I would have done so in any case, but I was nevertheless grateful for your advice last year.'

'Forgive me, Father, but I don't recall offering any advice last year. As for the matter of the *miai*, however, Noriko has indeed mentioned it to me a number of times. Indeed, she wrote to me soon after the *miai* expressing surprise at Father's . . . at Father's words about himself.'

'I dare say she was surprised. Noriko always did underestimate her old father. But I'm hardly the sort to allow my own daughter to suffer simply because I'm too proud to face up to things.'

'Noriko told me she was extremely puzzled by Father's behaviour that night. It seems the Saitos were equally puzzled. No one was at all sure what Father meant by it all. Indeed, Suichi also expressed his bewilderment when I read him Noriko's letter.'

'But this is extraordinary,' I said, laughing. 'Why, Setsuko, it was you yourself who pushed me to it last year. It was you who suggested I take "precautionary steps" so that we didn't slip up with the Saitos as we did with the Miyakes. Do you not remember?'

'No doubt I am being most forgetful, but I am afraid I have no recollection of what Father refers to.'

'Now, Setsuko, this is extraordinary.'

Setsuko suddenly stopped walking and exclaimed: 'How wonderful the maples look at this time of year!'

'Indeed,' I said. 'No doubt they'll look even better further into the autumn.'

'So wonderful,' my daughter said, smiling, and we began to walk again. Then she said: 'As a matter of fact, Father, it so happened that last night we were discussing one or two things, and Taro-san happened to mention a conversation he had had with you just last week. A conversation concerning the composer who recently committed suicide.'

'Yukio Naguchi? Ah yes, I remember that conversation. Now let me see, I believe Taro was suggesting the man's suicide was pointless.'

'Taro-san was somewhat concerned Father should be so interested in Mr Naguchi's death. Indeed, it would seem Father was drawing a comparison between Mr Naguchi's career and his own. We all felt concern at this news. In fact, we have all been somewhat concerned lately that Father is not becoming a little downhearted following his retirement.'

I laughed and said: 'You can put your mind at rest, Setsuko. I am not for one moment contemplating taking the sort of action Mr Naguchi did.'

'From what I understand,' she continued, 'Mr Naguchi's songs came to have enormous prevalence at every level of the war effort. There would thus appear to have been some substance to his wish that he should share responsibility along with the politicians and generals. But Father is wrong to even begin thinking in such terms about himself. Father was, after all, a painter.'

'Let me assure you, Setsuko, I wouldn't for a moment consider the sort of action Naguchi took. But then I am not too proud to see that I too was a man of some influence, who used that influence towards a disastrous end.'

My daughter seemed to consider this for a moment. Then she said:

'Forgive me, but it is perhaps important to see things in a proper perspective. Father painted some splendid pictures, and was no doubt most influential amongst other such painters. But Father's work had hardly to do with these larger matters of which we are speaking. Father was simply a painter. He must stop believing he has done some great wrong.'

'Well now, Setsuko, this is very different advice from last year. Then it seemed my career was a great liability.'

'Forgive me, Father, but I can only repeat I do not understand these references to the marriage negotiations last year. Indeed, it is some mystery to me why Father's career should have been of any particular relevance to the negotiations. The Saitos, it would seem, were certainly not concerned and, as we have said, they were very puzzled by Father's behaviour at the *miai*.'

'This is quite astonishing, Setsuko. The situation was that Dr Saito and I had been acquainted for a long time. As one of the city's most eminent art critics, he would have followed my career over the years and have been fully aware of its more regrettable aspects. It was therefore right and proper that I should make my attitude clear at that point in the proceedings. Indeed, I'm quite confident Dr Saito much appreciated my doing so.'

'Forgive me, but it would appear from what Taro-san has said that Dr Saito was never so familiar with Father's career. Of course, he always knew Father as a neighbour. But it would seem he was unaware that Father was connected with the art world at all until last year when the negotiations began.'

'You're quite wrong, Setsuko,' I said with a laugh. 'Dr Saito and I have known about each other for many years. We often used to stop in the street and exchange news about the art world.'

'No doubt then I am mistaken. Forgive me. But it is nevertheless important to stress that no one has ever considered Father's past something to view with recrimination. One hopes then that Father will cease to think of himself in terms of men like that unfortunate composer.'

I did not persist in arguing with Setsuko, and I seem to recall we soon moved on to discussing more casual topics. However, there is surely no doubt that my daughter was in error over much of what she asserted that morning. For one thing, it is impossible that Dr Saito could have been ignorant of my reputation as a painter for all those years. And when that evening after supper I contrived to get Taro to confirm this, I did so merely to make the point clear to Setsuko; for there was never any doubt in my mind. I have, for instance, the most vivid recollection of that sunny day some sixteen years ago when Dr Saito first addressed me as I stood adjusting the fence outside my new house. 'A great honour to have an artist of your stature in our neighbourhood,' he had said, recognizing my name on the gatepost. I remember that meeting quite clearly, and there can be no doubt that Setsuko is mistaken.

JUNE, 1950

After receiving the news of Matsuda's death late yesterday morning, I made myself a light lunch, then went out for a little exercise.

The day was pleasantly warm as I made my way down the hill. On reaching the river, I stepped up on to the Bridge of Hesitation and looked around me. The sky was a clear blue, and a little way down the bank, along where the new apartment blocks began, I could see two small boys playing with fishing poles at the water's edge. I watched them for some moments, turning over in my mind the news about Matsuda.

I had always meant to pay Matsuda further visits since re-establishing contact with him during Noriko's marriage negotiations, but in fact had not managed to get out to Arakawa again until just a month or so ago. I had gone on sheer impulse, having no idea at the time he was so near his end. Perhaps Matsuda would have died a little happier for having shared his thoughts with me that afternoon.

On my arrival at his house, Miss Suzuki had recognized me instantly and shown me in with some excitement. The way she did this seemed to suggest Matsuda had not had many callers since my visit eighteen months earlier.

'He's much stronger than the last time you were here,' she said happily.

I was shown into the reception room and a few moments later, Matsuda came in unaided, dressed in a loose kimono. He was clearly glad to see me again, and for some moments we talked of small matters and of mutual acquaintances. I believe it was not until Miss Suzuki had brought our tea and left again that I remembered to thank Matsuda for his letter of encouragement during my recent illness.

'You appear to have made a good recovery, Ono,' he remarked. 'To look at you, I'd never guess you'd been ill so recently.'

'I'm much better now,' I said. 'I have to be careful not to overexert myself. And I'm obliged to carry this stick around with me. Otherwise I feel as well as I ever did.'

'You disappoint me, Ono. And I thought we could be two old men discussing our ill health together. But here you are and it's just like the last time you came. I have to sit here and envy you your health.'

'Nonsense, Matsuda. You're looking very well.'

'You'll hardly convince me of that, Ono,' he said with a laugh, 'though it's true I've regained a little weight over this past year. But tell me, is Noriko-san happy? I heard her marriage went through successfully. When you last came here, you were very worried for her future.'

'Things have turned out very well. She's now expecting a child in the autumn. After all that worry, things have gone as well as I could ever have hoped for Noriko.'

'A grandchild in the autumn. Now that must be something to look forward to.'

'As a matter of fact,' I said, 'my elder daughter is expecting her second child next month. She's been longing for another child, so it's particularly good news.'

'Indeed, indeed. Two grandchildren to look forward to.' For a moment, he sat there smiling and nodding to himself. Then he said: 'No doubt you remember, Ono, I was always far too busy improving the world to think about marriage. Do you remember those arguments we used to have, just before you and Michiko-san were married?'

We both laughed.

'Two grandchildren,' Matsuda said again. 'Now, there's something to look forward to.'

'Indeed. I've been most fortunate as regards my daughters.'

'And tell me, Ono, are you painting these days?'

'A few watercolours to pass the time. Plants and flowers mostly, just for my own amusement.'

'I'm glad to hear you're painting again in any case. When you last came to see me, you seemed to have given up painting for good. You were very disillusioned then.'

'No doubt I was. I didn't touch paints for a long time.'

'Yes, Ono, you seemed very disillusioned.' Then he looked up at me with a smile and said: 'But then of course, you wanted so badly to make a grand contribution.'

I returned his smile, saying: 'But so did you, Matsuda. Your goals were no less grand. It was you, after all, who composed that manifesto for our China crisis campaign. Those were hardly the most modest of aspirations.'

We both laughed again. Then he said:

'No doubt you'll remember, Ono, how I used to call you naïve. How I used to tease you for your narrow artist's perspective. You used to get so angry with me. Well, it seems in the end neither of us had a broad enough view.'

'I suppose that's right. But if we'd seen things a little more clearly, then the likes of you and I me, Matsuda – who knows? – we may have done some real good. We had much energy and courage once. Indeed, we must have had plenty of both to conduct something like that New Japan campaign, you remember?'

'Indeed. There were some powerful forces set against us then. We might easily have lost our nerve. I suppose we must have been very determined, Ono.'

'But then I for one never saw things too clearly. A narrow artist's perspective, as you say. Why, even now, I find it hard to think of the world extending much beyond this city.'

'These days', Matsuda said, 'I find it hard to think of the world extending much beyond my garden. So perhaps you're the one with the wider perspective now, Ono.'

We laughed together once more, then Matsuda took a sip from his teacup.

'But there's no need to blame ourselves unduly,' he said.

'We at least acted on what we believed and did our utmost. It's just that in the end we turned out to be ordinary men. Ordinary men with no special gifts of insight. It was simply our misfortune to have been ordinary men during such times.'

Matsuda's earlier reference to his garden had drawn my attention in that direction. It was a mild spring afternoon, and Miss Suzuki had left a screen partially open, so that from where I sat I could see the sun reflected brightly on the polished boards of the veranda. A soft breeze was coming into the room, and with it a faint odour of smoke. I rose to my feet and went over to the screens.

'The smell of burning still makes me uneasy,' I remarked. 'It's not so long ago it meant bombings and fire.' I went on gazing out on to the garden for a moment, then added: 'Next month, it will be five years already since Michiko died.'

Matsuda remained silent for a while. Then I heard him say behind me:

'These days, a smell of burning usually means a neighbour is clearing his garden.'

Somewhere within the house, a clock began to chime.

'It's time to feed the carp,' Matsuda said. 'You know, I had to argue with Miss Suzuki for a long time before she would allow me to start feeding the carp again. I used to do it regularly, but then a few months ago, I tripped on one of those stepping stones. I had to argue with her a long time after that.'

Matsuda rose to his feet, and putting on some straw sandals left out on the veranda, we stepped down into the garden. The pond lay amidst sunshine at the far end of the garden and we proceeded with care along the stepping stones that ran across the smooth mounds of moss.

It was while we were standing at the edge of the pond, looking into the thick green water, that a sound made us both glance up. At a point not far from us, a small boy of about four or five was peering over the top of the garden fence, clinging with both arms to the branch of a tree. Matsuda smiled and called out:

'Ah, good afternoon, Botchan!'

The boy went on staring at us for a moment, then vanished. Matsuda smiled and began to throw feed into the water. 'Some neighbour's boy,' he said. 'Every day at this time, he climbs up on that tree trunk to watch me come out and feed my fish. But he's shy and if I try and speak to him he runs away.' He gave a small laugh to himself. 'I often wonder why he makes the effort like that every day. There's nothing much for him to see. Just an old man with a stick, standing by his pond feeding the carp. I wonder what he finds so fascinating in such a scene.'

I looked over to the fence again to where a moment ago the small face had been, and said: 'Well, today he got a surprise. Today, he saw two old men with sticks, standing by the pond.'

Matsuda laughed happily and went on throwing feed into the water. Two or three splendid carp had come to the surface, their scales glistening in the sunlight.

'Army officers, politicians, businessmen,' Matsuda said. 'They've all been blamed for what happened to this country. But as for the likes of us, Ono, our contribution was always marginal. No one cares now what the likes of you and me once did. They look at us and see only two old men with their sticks.' He smiled at me, then went on feeding the fish. 'We're the only ones who care now. The likes of you and me, Ono, when we look back over our lives and see they were flawed, we're the only ones who care now.'

But even as he uttered such words, there remained something in Matsuda's manner that afternoon to suggest he was anything but a disillusioned man. And surely there was no reason for him to have died disillusioned. He may indeed have looked back over his life and seen certain flaws, but surely he would have recognized also those aspects he could feel proud of. For, as he pointed out himself, the likes of him and me, we have the satisfaction of knowing that whatever we did, we did at the time in the best of faith. Of course, we took some bold steps and often did things with much single-mindedness; but this is surely preferable to never putting one's convictions to the test, for lack of will or courage. When one holds convictions deeply enough, there surely comes a point when it is despicable to prevaricate further. I feel confident Matsuda would have thought along these same lines when looking back over his life.

There is a particular moment I often bring to my mind – it was in the May of 1938, just after I had been presented with the Shigeta Foundation Award. By that point in my career I had received various awards and honours, but the Shigeta Foundation Award was in most people's view a major milestone. In addition, as I recall, we had finished that same week our New Japan campaign, which had proved a great success. The night after the presentation, then, was one of much celebrating. I remember sitting in the Migi-Hidari, surrounded by my pupils and various of my colleagues, being plied with drink, listening to speech after speech in tribute to me. All manner of acquaintances called in to the Migi-Hidari that night to offer their congratulations; I even recall a chief of police I had never met before coming in to pay his respects. But happy as I was that night, the feeling of deep triumph and fulfilment which the award should have brought was curiously missing. In fact, I was not to experience such a feeling until a few days later, when I was out in the hilly countryside of the Wakaba province.

I had not been back to Wakaba for some sixteen years – not since that day I had left Mori-san's villa, determined, but nevertheless fearful that the future held nothing for me. Over the course of those years, though I had broken all formal contacts with Mori-san, I had remained curious of any news concerning my old teacher, and so was fully aware of the steady decline of his reputation in the city. His endeavours to bring European influence into the Utamaro tradition had come to be regarded as fundamentally unpatriotic, and he would be heard of from time to time holding struggling exhibitions at ever less prestigious venues. In fact, I had heard from more that one source that he had begun illustrating popular magazines to maintain his income. At the same time, I could be quite confident Mori-san had followed the course of my career and there was every chance he had heard of my receiving the Shigeta Foundation Award. It was then with a keen awareness of the changes time had brought on us that I stepped off the train at the village station that day.

It was a sunny spring afternoon as I set off towards Mori-san's villa along those hilly paths through the woodland. I went slowly, savouring the experience of that walk I had once known so well. And all the while I turned over in my mind what might occur when I came face to face with Mori-san once more. Perhaps he would receive me as an honoured guest; or perhaps he would be as cold and distant as during my final days at the villa; then again, he might behave towards me in much the way he had always done while I had been his favourite pupil – that is, as though the great changes in our respective status had not occurred. The last of these possibilities struck me as the most likely and I remember considering how I would respond. I would not, I resolved, revert to old habits and address him as 'Sensei'; instead, I would simply address him as though he were a colleague. And if he persisted in failing to acknowledge the position I now occupied, I would say, with a friendly laugh, something to the effect of: 'As you see, Mori-san, I have not been obliged to spend my time illustrating comic books as you once feared.'

In time I found myself at that spot on the high mountain path that gave a fine view of the villa standing amongst trees in the hollow below. I paused a moment to admire that view, as I had often done years before. There was a refreshing wind, and down in the hollow, I could see the trees swaying gently. I wondered to myself if the villa had been renovated, but it was impossible to ascertain from such a distance.

After a while, I seated myself amidst the wild grass growing along the ridge and went on gazing at Mori-san's villa. I had bought some oranges at a stall by the village station, and taking these from my kerchief, I began to eat them one by one. And it was as I sat there, looking down at the villa, enjoying the taste of those fresh oranges, that that deep sense of triumph and satisfaction began to rise within me. It is hard to describe the feeling, for it was quite different from the sort of elation one feels from smaller triumphs – and, as I say, quite different from anything I had experienced during the celebrations at the Migi-Hidari. It was a profound sense of happiness deriving from the conviction that one's efforts have been justified; that the hard work undertaken, the doubts overcome, have all been worthwhile; that one has achieved something of real value and distinction. I did not go any further towards the villa that day – it seemed quite pointless. I simply continued to sit there for an hour or so, in deep contentment, eating my oranges.

It is not, I fancy, a feeling many people will come to experience. The likes of the Tortoise – the likes of Shintaro – they may plod on, competent and inoffensive, but their kind will never know the sort of happiness I felt that day. For their kind do not know what it is to risk everything in the endeavour to rise above the mediocre.

Matsuda, though, was a different case. Although he and I often quarrelled, our approaches to life were identical, and I am confident he would have been able to look back on one or two such moments. Indeed, I am sure he was thinking along these lines when he said to me that last time we spoke, a gentle smile on his face: 'We at least acted on what we believed and did our utmost.' For however one may come in later years to reassess one's achievements, it is always a consolation to know that one's life has contained a moment or two or real satisfaction such as I experienced that day up on that high mountain path.

Yesterday morning, after standing on the Bridge of

Hesitation for some moments thinking about Matsuda, I walked on to where our pleasure district used to be. The area has now been rebuilt and has become quite unrecognizable. The narrow little street that once ran through the centre of the district, crowded with people and the cloth banners of the various establishments, has now been replaced by a wide concrete road along which heavy trucks come and go all day. Where Mrs Kawakami's stood, there is now a glass-fronted office building, four storeys high. Neighbouring it are more such large buildings, and during the day, one can see office workers, delivery men, messengers, all moving busily in and out of them. There are no bars now until one reaches Furu-kawa, but here and there, one may recognize a piece of fencing or else a tree, left over from the old days, looking oddly incongruous in its new setting.

Where the Migi-Hidari once stood is now a front yard for a group of offices set back from the road. Some of the senior employees leave their cars in this yard, but it is for the most part a clear space of tarmac with a few young trees planted at various points. At the front of this yard, facing the road, there is a bench of the sort one may find in a park. For whose benefit it has been placed there, I do not know, for I have never seen any of these busy people ever stopping to relax on it. But it is my fancy that the bench occupies a spot very close to where our old table in the Migi-Hidari would have been situated, and I have taken at times to sitting on it. It may well not be a public bench, but then it is close to the pavement, and no one has ever objected to my sitting there. Yesterday morning, with the sun shining pleasantly, I sat down on it again and remained there for a while, observing the activity around me.

It must have been approaching the lunch hour by then, for across the road I could see groups of employees in their bright white shirtsleeves emerging from the glass-fronted building where Mrs Kawakami's used to be. And as I watched, I was struck by how full of optimism and enthusiasm these young people were. At one point, two young men leaving the building stopped to talk with a third who was on his way in. They stood on the doorsteps of that glass-fronted building, laughing together in the sunshine. One young man, whose face I could see most clearly, was laughing in a particularly cheerful manner, with something of the open innocence of a child. Then with a quick gesture, the three colleagues parted and went their ways.

I smiled to myself as I watched these young office workers from my bench. Of course, at times, when I remember those brightly-lit bars and all those people gathered beneath the lamps, laughing a little more boisterously perhaps than those young men yesterday, but with much the same good-heartedness, I feel a certain nostalgia for the past and the district as it used to be. But to see how our city has been rebuilt, how things have recovered so rapidly over these years, fills me with genuine gladness. Our nation, it seems, whatever mistakes it may have made in the past, has now another chance to make a better go of things. One can only wish these young people well.